Joseph Lewis French

Ghost Stories

Leseklassiker

Joseph Lewis French

Ghost Stories

ISBN/EAN: 9783955630393

Auflage: 1

Erscheinungsjahr: 2013

Erscheinungsort: Bremen, Deutschland

Leseklassiker

Foreword

The ghost story is as old as human speech, — and perhaps even antedates it. A naïve acceptance of the supernatural was unquestionably one of the primal attributes of human intelligence. The ghost story may thus quite conceivably be the first form of tale ever invented. It makes its appearance comparatively early in the annals of literature. Who that has read it is likely to forget Pliny's account in a letter to an intimate of an apparition shortly after death to a mutual acquaintance? Old books of tales and legends are full of the ghost story. It has persisted throughout the ages. It began to attain some real standing in literature, — to take its definite place, — a little more than a century ago. Like the apparition it embodies it had always been — and is still to-day even — more or less discredited. Mrs. Radcliffe gave it a new being and even a certain dignity in her "Castle of Otranto"; and after her came Sir Walter Scott who frankly surrendered to the power and charm of the theme. The line of succession has been continuous. The ghost has held his own with his human fellow in fiction, and his tale has been told with increasing skill as the art of the writer has developed. To-day the case for the ghost as an element in fiction is an exceedingly strong one. There has indeed sprung into being within a couple of decades a new school of such writers. Nowadays almost every fictionist of account produces one good thriller at least of this sort. The temptation is irresistible for the simple reason that the theme imposes absolutely no limit on the imagination.

The reader will find here a careful selection illustrating the growth in art of this exotic in literature during the past fifty years, and for a contrast, spanning the centuries, the naïve narration of Pliny the Younger.

Joseph Lewis French.

Contents

I. The Listener — Algernon Blackwood

Sept. 4. — I have hunted all over London for rooms suited to my income — £120 a year — and have at last found them. Two rooms, without modern conveniences, it is true, and in an old, ramshackle building, but within a stone's throw of P — Place and in an eminently respectable street. The rent is only £25 a year. I had begun to despair when at last I found them by chance. The chance was a mere chance, and unworthy of record. I had to sign a lease for a year, and I did so willingly. The furniture from our old place in H — shire, which has been stored so long, will just suit them.

*****

Oct. 1. — Here I am in my two rooms, in the centre of London, and not far from the offices of the periodicals where occasionally I dispose of an article or two. The building is at the end of a *cul-de-sac*. The alley is well paved and clean, and lined chiefly with the backs of sedate and institutional-looking buildings. There is a stable in it. My own house is dignified with the title of "Chambers." I feel as if one day the honour must prove too much for it, and it will swell with pride — and fall asunder. It is very old. The floor of my sitting-room has valleys and low hills on it, and the top of the door slants away from the ceiling with a glorious disregard of what is usual. They must have quarrelled — fifty years ago — and have been going apart ever since.

*****

Oct. 2. — My landlady is old and thin, with a faded, dusty face. She is uncommunicative. The few words she utters seem to cost her pain. Probably her lungs are half choked with dust. She keeps my rooms as free from this commodity as possible, and has the assistance of a strong girl who brings up the breakfast and lights the fire. As I have said already, she is not communicative. In reply to pleasant efforts on my part she informed me briefly that I was the only occupant of the house at present. My rooms had not been occupied for some years. There had been other gentlemen upstairs, but they had left.

She never looks straight at me when she speaks, but fixes her dim eyes on my middle waistcoat button, till I get nervous and begin to think it isn't on straight, or is the wrong sort of button altogether.

*****

Oct. 8. — My week's book is nicely kept, and so far is reasonable. Milk and sugar 7d., bread 6d., butter 8d., marmalade 6d., eggs 1s. 8d., laundress 2s. 9d., oil 6d., attendance 5s.; total 12s. 2d.

The landlady has a son who, she told me, is "somethink on a homnibus." He comes occasionally to see her. I think he drinks, for he talks very loud, regardless of the hour of the day or night, and tumbles about over the furniture downstairs.

All the morning I sit indoors writing — articles; verses for the comic papers; a novel I've been "at" for three years, and concerning which I have dreams; a children's book, in which the imagination has free rein; and another book which is to last as long as myself, since it is an honest record of my soul's advance or retreat in the struggle of life. Besides these, I keep a book of poems which I use as a safety valve, and concerning which I have no dreams whatsoever. Between the lot I am always occupied. In the afternoons I generally try to take a walk for my health's sake, through

Regent's Park, into Kensington Gardens, or farther afield to Hampstead Heath.

*****

Oct. 10. — Everything went wrong to-day. I have two eggs for breakfast. This morning one of them was bad. I rang the bell for Emily. When she came in I was reading the paper, and, without looking up, I said, "Egg's bad." "Oh, is it, sir?" she said; "I'll get another one," and went out, taking the egg with her. I waited my breakfast for her return, which was in five minutes. She put the new egg on the table and went away. But, when I looked down, I saw that she had taken away the good egg and left the bad one — all green and yellow — in the slop basin. I rang again.

"You've taken the wrong egg," I said.

"Oh!" she exclaimed; "I thought the one I took down didn't smell so *very* bad." In due time she returned with the good egg, and I resumed my breakfast with two eggs, but less appetite. It was all very trivial, to be sure, but so stupid that I felt annoyed. The character of that egg influenced everything I did. I wrote a bad article, and tore it up. I got a bad headache. I used bad words — to myself. Everything was bad, so I "chucked" work and went for a long walk.

I dined at a cheap chop-house on my way back, and reached home about nine o'clock.

Rain was just beginning to fall as I came in, and the wind was rising. It promised an ugly night. The alley looked dismal and dreary, and the hall of the house, as I passed through it, felt chilly as a tomb. It was the first stormy night I had experienced in my new quarters. The draughts were awful. They came criss-cross, met in the middle of the room, and formed eddies and whirlpools and cold silent currents that almost lifted the hair of my head. I stuffed up the sashes of the windows with neckties and odd socks, and sat over the smoky fire to keep warm. First I tried to write, but found it too cold. My hand turned to ice on the paper.

What tricks the wind did play with the old place! It came rushing up the forsaken alley with a sound like the feet of a hurrying crowd of people who stopped suddenly at the door. I felt as if a lot of curious folk had arranged themselves just outside and were staring up at my windows. Then they took to their heels again and fled whispering and laughing down the lane, only, however, to return with the next gust of wind and repeat their impertinence. On the other side of my room, a single square window opens into a sort of shaft, or well, that measures about six feet across to the back wall of another house. Down this funnel the wind dropped, and puffed and shouted. Such noises I never heard before. Between these two entertainments I sat over the fire in a greatcoat, listening to the deep booming in the chimney. It was like being in a ship at sea, and I almost looked for the floor to rise in undulations and rock to and fro.

*****

Oct. 12. — I wish I were not quite so lonely — and so poor. And yet I love both my loneliness and my poverty. The former makes me appreciate the companionship of the wind and rain, while the latter preserves my liver and prevents me wasting time in dancing attendance upon women. Poor, ill-dressed men are not acceptable "attendants."

My parents are dead, and my only sister is — no, not dead exactly, but married to a very rich man. They travel most of the time, he to find his health, she to lose herself. Through sheer neglect on her part she has long passed out of my life. The door closed when, after an absolute silence of five years, she sent me a cheque for £50 at Christmas. It was signed by her husband! I returned it to her in a thousand pieces and in an unstamped envelope. So at least I had the satisfaction of knowing that it cost her something! She wrote back with a broad quill pen that covered a whole page with three lines, "You are evidently as cracked as ever, and rude and ungrateful into the bargain." It had always been my special terror lest the insanity in my father's family should leap across the generations and appear in me. This thought haunted me, and she knew it. So after this little exchange of civilities the door slammed, never to open again. I heard the crash it made, and, with it, the falling from the walls of my heart of many little bits of china with their own peculiar value — rare china, some of it, that only needed dusting. The same walls, too, carried mirrors in which I used sometimes to see reflected the misty lawns of childhood, the daisy chains, the wind-torn blossoms scattered through the orchard by warm rains, the robbers' cave in the long walk, and the hidden store of apples in the hay-loft. She was my inseparable companion then — but, when the door slammed, the mirrors cracked across their entire length, and the visions they held vanished for ever. Now I am quite alone. At forty one cannot begin all over again to build up careful friendships, and all others are comparatively worthless.

*****

Oct. 14. — My bedroom is 10 by 10. It is below the level of the front room, and a step leads down into it. Both rooms are very quiet on calm nights, for there is no traffic down this forsaken alley-way. In spite of the occasional larks of the wind, it is a most sheltered strip. At its upper end, below my windows, all the cats of the neighbourhood congregate as soon as darkness gathers. They lie undisturbed on the long ledge of a blind window of the opposite building, for after the postman has come and gone at 9:30, no footsteps ever dare to interrupt their sinister conclave, no step but my own, or sometimes the unsteady footfall of the son who "is somethink on a homnibus."

*****

Oct. 15. — I dined at an "A. B. C." shop on poached eggs and coffee, and then went for a stroll round the outer edge of Regent's Park. It was ten o'clock when I got home. I counted no less than thirteen cats, all of a dark colour, crouching under the lee side of the alley walls. It was a cold night, and the stars shone like points of ice in a blue-black sky. The cats turned their heads and stared at me in silence as I passed. An odd sensation of shyness took possession of me under the glare of so many pairs of unblinking eyes. As I fumbled with the latch-key they jumped noiselessly down and pressed against my legs, as if anxious to be let in. But I slammed the door in their faces and ran quickly upstairs. The front room, as I entered to grope for the matches, felt as cold as a stone vault, and the air held an unusual dampness.

*****

Oct. 17. — For several days I have been working on a ponderous article that allows no play for the fancy. My imagination requires a judicious rein; I am afraid to let it loose, for it carries me sometimes into appalling places beyond the stars and beneath the world. No one realizes the danger more than I do. But what a foolish thing to write here — for there is no one to know, no one to realize! My mind of late has held unusual thoughts, thoughts I have never had before, about medicines and drugs and the treatment of strange illnesses. I cannot imagine their source. At no time in my life have I dwelt upon such ideas as now constantly throng my brain. I have had no exercise lately, for the weather has been shocking; and all my afternoons have been spent in the reading-room of the British Museum, where I have a reader's ticket.

I have made an unpleasant discovery: there are rats in the house. At night from my bed I have heard them scampering across the hills and valleys of the front room, and my sleep has been a good deal disturbed in consequence.

*****

Oct. 24. — Last night the son who is "somethink on a homnibus" came in. He had evidently been drinking, for I heard loud and angry voices below in the kitchen long after I had gone to bed. Once, too, I caught the singular words rising up to me through the floor, "Burning from top to bottom is the only thing that'll ever make this 'ouse right." I knocked on the floor, and the voices ceased suddenly, though later I again heard their clamour in my dreams.

These rooms are very quiet, almost too quiet sometimes. On windless nights they are silent as the grave, and the house might be miles in the country. The roar of London's traffic reaches me only in heavy, distant vibrations. It holds an ominous note sometimes, like that of an approaching army, or an immense tidal-wave very far away thundering in the night.

*****

Oct. 27. — Mrs. Monson, though admirably silent, is a foolish, fussy woman. She does such stupid things. In dusting the room she puts all my things in the wrong places. The ash-trays, which should be on the writing-table she sets in a silly row on the mantelpiece. The pen-tray, which should be beside the inkstand, she hides away cleverly among the books on my reading-desk. My gloves she arranges daily in idiotic array upon a half-filled bookshelf, and I always have to rearrange them on the low table by the door. She places my armchair at impossible angles between the fire and the light, and the tablecloth — the one with Trinity Hall stains — she puts on the table in such a fashion that when I look at it I feel as if my tie and all my clothes were on crooked and awry. She exasperates me. Her very silence and meekness are irritating. Sometimes I feel inclined to throw the inkstand at her, just to bring an expression into her watery eyes and a squeak from those colourless lips. Dear me! What violent expressions I am making use of! How very foolish of me! And yet it almost seems as if the words were not my own, but had been spoken into my ear — I mean, I never make use of such terms naturally.

*****

Oct. 30. — I have been here a month. The place does not agree with me, I think. My headaches are more frequent and violent, and my nerves are a perpetual source of discomfort and annoyance.

I have conceived a great dislike for Mrs. Monson, a feeling I am certain she reciprocates. Somehow, the impression comes frequently to me that there are goings on in this house of which I know nothing, and which she is careful to hide from me.

Last night her son slept in the house, and this morning as I was standing at the window I saw him go out. He glanced up and caught my eye. It was a loutish figure and a singularly repulsive face that I saw, and he gave me the benefit of a very unpleasant leer. At least, so I imagined.

*****

Nov. 2. — The utter stillness of this house is beginning to oppress me. I wish there were other fellows living upstairs. No footsteps ever sound overhead, and no tread ever passes my door to go up the next flight of stairs. I am beginning to feel some curiosity to go up myself and see what the upper rooms are like. I feel lonely here and isolated, swept into a deserted corner of the world and forgotten.... Once I actually caught myself gazing into the long, cracked mirrors, trying to see the sunlight dancing beneath the trees in the orchard. But only deep shadows seemed to congregate there now, and I soon desisted.

It has been very dark all day, and no wind stirring. The fogs have begun. I had to use a reading-lamp all this morning. There was no cart to be heard to-day. I actually missed it. This morning, in the gloom and silence, I think I could almost have welcomed it. After all, the sound is a very human one, and this empty house at the end of the alley holds other noises that are not quite so satisfactory.

I have never once seen a policeman in the lane, and the postmen always hurry out with no evidence of a desire to loiter.

10 P.M. — As I write this I hear no sound but the deep murmur of the distant traffic and the low sighing of the wind. The two sounds melt into one another. Now and again a cat raises its shrill, uncanny

cry upon the darkness. The cats are always there under my windows when the darkness falls. The wind is dropping into the funnel with a noise like the sudden sweeping of immense distant wings. It is a dreary night. I feel lost and forgotten.

*****

Nov. 3. — From my windows I can see arrivals. When anyone comes to the door I can just see the hat and shoulders and the hand on the bell. Only two fellows have been to see me since I came here two months ago. Both of them I saw from the window before they came up, and heard their voices asking if I was in. Neither of them ever came back.

I have finished the ponderous article. On reading it through, however, I was dissatisfied with it, and drew my pencil through almost every page. There were strange expressions and ideas in it that I could not explain, and viewed with amazement, not to say alarm. They did not sound like my *very own,* and I could not remember having written them. Can it be that my memory is beginning to be affected?

My pens are never to be found. That stupid old woman puts them in a different place each day. I must give her due credit for finding so many new hiding places; such ingenuity is wonderful. I have told her repeatedly, but she always says, "I'll speak to Emily, sir." Emily always says, "I'll tell Mrs. Monson, sir." Their foolishness makes me irritable and scatters all my thoughts. I should like to stick the lost pens into them and turn them out, blind-eyed, to be scratched and mauled by those thousand hungry cats. Whew! What a ghastly thought! Where in the world did it come from? Such an idea is no more my own than it is the policeman's. Yet I felt I *had* to write it. It was like a voice singing in my head, and my pen wouldn't stop till the last word was finished. What ridiculous nonsense! I must and will restrain myself. I must take more regular exercise; my nerves and liver plague me horribly.

*****

Nov. 4. — I attended a curious lecture in the French quarter on "Death," but the room was so hot and I was so weary that I fell asleep. The only part I heard, however, touched my imagination vividly. Speaking of suicides, the lecturer said that self-murder was no escape from the miseries of the present, but only a preparation of greater sorrow for the future. Suicides, he declared, cannot shirk their responsibilities so easily. They must return to take up life exactly where they laid it so violently down, but with the added pain and punishment of their weakness. Many of them wander the earth in unspeakable misery till they can *reclothe* themselves in the body of some one else — generally a lunatic or weak-minded person, who cannot resist the hideous obsession. This is their only means of escape. Surely a weird and horrible idea! I wish I had slept all the time and not heard it at all. My mind is morbid enough without such ghastly fancies. Such mischievous propaganda should be stopped by the police. I'll write to the *Times* and suggest it. Good idea!

I walked home through Greek Street, Soho, and imagined that a hundred years had slipped back into place and De Quincey was still there, haunting the night with invocations to his "just, subtle, and mighty" drug. His vast dreams seemed to hover not very far away. Once started in my brain, the pictures refused to go away; and I saw him sleeping in that cold, tenantless mansion with the strange little waif who was afraid of its ghosts, both together in the shadows under a single horseman's cloak; or wandering in the companionship of the spectral Anne; or, later still, on his way to the eternal rendezvous she never was able to keep. What an unutterable gloom, what an untold horror of sorrow and suffering comes over me as I try to realize something of what that man — boy he then was — must have taken into his lonely heart.

As I came up the alley I saw a light in the top window, and a head and shoulders thrown in an exaggerated shadow upon the blind. I wondered what the son could be doing up there at such an hour.

*****

Nov. 5. — This morning, while writing, some one came up the creaking stairs and knocked cautiously at my door. Thinking it was the landlady, I said, "Come in!" The knock was repeated, and I cried louder, "Come in, come in!" But no one turned the handle, and I continued my writing with a vexed "Well, stay out, then!" under my breath. Went on writing. I tried to, but my thoughts had suddenly dried up at their source. I could not set down a single word. It was a dark, yellow-fog morning, and there was little enough inspiration in the air as it was, but that stupid woman standing just outside my door waiting to be told again to come in roused a spirit of vexation that filled my head to the exclusion of all else. At last I jumped up and opened the door myself.

"What do you want, and why in the world don't you come in?" I cried out. But the words dropped into empty air. There was no one there. The fog poured up the dingy staircase in deep yellow coils, but there was no sign of a human being anywhere.

I slammed the door, with imprecations upon the

house and its noises, and went back to my work. A few minutes later Emily came in with a letter.

"Were you or Mrs. Monson outside a few minutes ago knocking at my door?"

"No, sir."

"Are you sure?"

"Mrs. Monson's gone to market, and there's no one but me and the child in the 'ole 'ouse, and I've been washing the dishes for the last hour, sir."

I fancied the girl's face turned a shade paler. She fidgeted toward the door with a glance over her shoulder.

"Wait, Emily," I said, and then told her what I had heard. She stared stupidly at me, though her eyes shifted now and then over the articles in the room.

"Who was it?" I asked when I had come to the end.

"Mrs. Monson says it's honly mice," she said, as if repeating a learned lesson.

"Mice!" I exclaimed; "it's nothing of the sort. Someone was feeling about outside my door. Who was it? Is the son in the house?"

Her whole manner changed suddenly, and she became earnest instead of evasive. She seemed anxious to tell the truth.

"Oh, no, sir; there's no one in the house at all but you and me and the child, and there couldn't have been nobody at your door. As for them knocks — " She stopped abruptly, as though she had said too much.

"Well, what about the knocks?" I said more gently.

"Of course," she stammered, "the knocks isn't mice, nor the footsteps neither, but then — " Again she came to a full halt.

"Anything wrong with the house?"

"Lor', no, sir; the drains is splendid."

"I don't mean drains, girl. I mean, did anything — anything bad ever happen here?"

She flushed up to the roots of her hair, and then turned suddenly pale again. She was obviously in considerable distress, and there was something she was anxious, yet afraid to tell — some forbidden thing she was not allowed to mention.

"I don't mind what it was, only I should like to know," I said encouragingly.

Raising her frightened eyes to my face, she began to blurt out something about "that which 'appened once to a gentleman that lived hupstairs," when a shrill voice calling her name sounded below.

"Emily, Emily!" It was the returning landlady, and the girl tumbled downstairs as if pulled backward by a rope, leaving me full of conjectures as to what in the world could have happened to a gentleman *upstairs* that could in so curious a manner affect my ears *downstairs*.

*****

Nov. 10. — I have done capital work; have finished the ponderous article and had it accepted for the — — *Review*, and another one ordered. I feel well and cheerful, and have had regular exercise and good sleep; no headaches, no nerves, no liver! Those pills the chemist recommended are wonderful. Even the gray-faced landlady rouses pity in me; I am sorry for her: so worn, so weary, so oddly put together, just like the building. She looks as if she had once suffered some shock of terror, and was momentarily dreading another. When I spoke to her to-day very gently about not putting the pens in the ash-tray and the gloves on the book-shelf she raised her faint eyes to mine for the first time, and said with the ghost of a smile, "I'll try and remember, sir," I felt inclined to pat her on the back and say, "Come, cheer up and be jolly. Life's not so bad after all." Oh! I am much better. There's nothing like open air and success and good sleep. They build up as if by magic the portions of the heart eaten down by despair and unsatisfied yearnings. Even to the cats I feel friendly. When I came in at eleven o'clock to-night they followed me to the door in a stream, and I stooped down to stroke the one nearest to me. Bah! The brute hissed and spat, and struck at me with her paws. The claw caught my hand and drew blood in a thin line. The others danced sideways into the darkness, screeching, as though I had done them an injury. I believe these cats really hate me. Perhaps they are only waiting to be reinforced. Then they will attack me. Ha, ha! In spite of the momentary annoyance, this fancy sent me laughing upstairs to my room.

The fire was out, and the room seemed unusually cold. As I groped my way over to the mantelpiece to find the matches I realized all at once that there was another person standing beside me in the darkness. I could, of course, see nothing, but my fingers, feeling along the ledge, came into forcible contact with something that was at once withdrawn. It was cold and moist. I could have sworn it was somebody's hand.

My flesh began to creep instantly.

"Who's that?" I exclaimed in a loud voice.

My voice dropped into the silence like a pebble into a deep well. There was no answer, but at the same moment I heard someone moving away from me across the room in the direction of the door. It was a confused sort of footstep, and the sound of garments brushing the furniture on the way. The same second my hand stumbled upon the matchbox, and I struck a light. I expected to see Mrs. Monson, or Emily, or perhaps the son who is something on an omnibus. But the flare of the gas jet illumined an empty room; there was not a sign of a person anywhere. I felt the hair stir upon my head, and instinctively I backed up against the wall, lest something should approach me from behind. I was distinctly alarmed. But the next minute I recovered myself. The door was open on to the landing, and I crossed the room, not without some inward trepidation, and went out. The light from the room fell upon the stairs, but there was no one to be seen anywhere, nor was there any sound on the creaking wooden staircase to indicate a departing creature.

I was in the act of turning to go in again when a sound overhead caught my ear. It was a very faint sound, not unlike the sigh of wind; yet it could not have been the wind, for the night was still as the grave. Though it was not repeated, I resolved to go upstairs and see for myself what it all meant. Two senses had been affected — touch and hearing — and I could not believe that I had been deceived. So, with a lighted candle, I went stealthily forth on my unpleasant journey into the upper regions of this queer little old house.

On the first landing there was only one door, and

it was locked. On the second there was also only one door, but when I turned the handle it opened. There came forth to meet me the chill musty air that is characteristic of a long unoccupied room. With it there came an indescribable odour. I use the adjective advisedly. Though very faint, diluted as it were, it was nevertheless an odour that made my gorge rise. I had never smelt anything like it before, and I cannot describe it.

The room was small and square, close under the roof, with a sloping ceiling and two tiny windows. It was cold as the grave, without a shred of carpet or a stick of furniture. The icy atmosphere and the nameless odour combined to make the room abominable to me, and, after lingering a moment to see that it contained no cupboards or corners into which a person might have crept for concealment, I made haste to shut the door, and went downstairs again to bed. Evidently I had been deceived after all as to the noise.

In the night I had a foolish but very vivid dream. I dreamed that the landlady and another person, dark and not properly visible, entered my room on all fours, followed by a horde of immense cats. They attacked me as I lay in bed, and murdered me, and then dragged my body upstairs and deposited it on the floor of that cold little square room under the roof.

*****

Nov. 11. — Since my talk with Emily — the unfinished talk — I have hardly once set eyes on her. Mrs. Monson now attends wholly to my wants. As usual, she does everything exactly as I don't like it done. It is all too utterly trivial to mention, but it is exceedingly irritating. Like small doses of morphine often repeated she has finally a cumulative effect.

*****

Nov. 12. — This morning I woke early, and came into the front room to get a book, meaning to read in bed till it was time to get up. Emily was laying the fire.

"Good morning!" I said cheerfully. "Mind you make a good fire. It's very cold."

The girl turned and showed me a startled face. It was not Emily at all!

"Where's Emily?" I exclaimed.

"You mean the girl as was 'ere before me?"

"Has Emily left?"

"I came on the 6th," she replied sullenly, "and she'd gone then." I got my book and went back to bed. Emily must have been sent away almost immediately after our conversation. This reflection kept coming between me and the printed page. I was glad when it was time to get up. Such prompt energy, such merciless decision, seemed to argue something of importance — to somebody.

*****

Nov. 13. — The wound inflicted by the cat's claw has swollen, and causes me annoyance and some pain. It throbs and itches. I'm afraid my blood must be in poor condition, or it would have healed by now. I opened it with a penknife soaked in an antiseptic solution, and cleaned it thoroughly. I have heard unpleasant stories of the results of wounds inflicted by cats.

*****

Nov. 14. — In spite of the curious effect this

house certainly exercises upon my nerves, I like it. It is lonely and deserted in the very heart of London, but it is also for that reason quiet to work in. I wonder why it is so cheap. Some people might be suspicious, but I did not even ask the reason. No answer is better than a lie. If only I could remove the cats from the outside and the rats from the inside. I feel that I shall grow accustomed more and more to its peculiarities, and shall die here. Ah, that expression reads queerly and gives a wrong impression: I meant *live and die* here. I shall renew the lease from year to year till one of us crumbles to pieces. From present indications the building will be the first to go.

*****

Nov. 16. — This morning I woke to find my clothes scattered about the room, and a cane chair overturned beside the bed. My coat and waistcoat looked just as if they had been *tried on* by someone in the night. I had horribly vivid dreams, too, in which someone covering his face with his hands kept coming close up to me, crying out as if in pain, "Where can I find covering? Oh, who will clothe me?" How silly, and yet it frightened me a little. It was so dreadfully real. It is now over a year since I last walked in my sleep and woke up with such a shock on the cold pavement of Earl's Court Road, where I then lived. I thought I was cured, but evidently not. This discovery has rather a disquieting effect upon me. To-night I shall resort to the old trick of tying my toe to the bed-post.

*****

Nov. 17. — Last night I was again troubled by most oppressive dreams. Someone seemed to be moving in the night up and down my room, sometimes passing into the front room, and then returning to stand beside the bed and stare intently down upon me. I was being watched by this person all night long. I never actually awoke, though I was often very near it. I suppose it was a nightmare from indigestion, for this morning I have one of my old vile headaches. Yet all my clothes lay about the floor when I awoke, where they had evidently been flung (had I tossed them?) during the dark hours, and my trousers trailed over the step into the front room.

Worse than this, though — I fancied I noticed about the room in the morning that strange, fetid odour. Though very faint, its mere suggestion is foul and nauseating. What in the world can it be, I wonder?... In future I shall lock my door.

*****

Nov. 26. — I have accomplished a lot of good work during this past week, and have also managed to get regular exercise. I have felt well and in an equable state of mind. Only two things have occurred to disturb my equanimity. The first is trivial in itself, and no doubt to be easily explained. The upper window where I saw the light on the night of November 4, with the shadow of a large head and shoulder upon the blind, is one of the windows in the square room under the roof. In reality it has *no blind at all*!

Here is the other thing. I was coming home last night in a fresh fall of snow about eleven o'clock, my umbrella low down over my head. Half-way up the alley, where the snow was wholly untrodden, I saw a man's legs in front of me. The umbrella hid the rest of his figure, but on raising it I saw that he was tall and broad and was walking, as I was, towards the door of my house. He could not have been four feet ahead of me. I had thought the alley was empty when I entered it, but might of course been mistaken very easily.

A sudden gust of wind compelled me to lower the umbrella, and when I raised it again, not half a minute later, there was no longer any man to be seen. With a few more steps I reached the door. It was closed as usual. I then noticed with a sudden sensation of dismay that the surface of the freshly fallen snow was *unbroken*. My own footmarks were the only ones to be seen anywhere, and though I retraced my way to the point where I had first seen the man, I could find no slightest impression of any other boots. Feeling creepy and uncomfortable, I went upstairs, and was glad to get into bed.

*****

Nov. 28. – With the fastening of my bedroom door the disturbances ceased. I am convinced that I walked in my sleep. Probably I untied my toe and then tied it up again. The fancied security of the locked door would alone have been enough to restore sleep to my troubled spirit and enable me to rest quietly.

Last night, however, the annoyance was suddenly renewed in another and more aggressive form. I woke in the darkness with the impression that some one was standing outside my bedroom door *listening*. As I became more awake the impression grew into positive knowledge. Though there was no appreciable sound of moving or breathing, I was so convinced of the propinquity of a listener that I crept out of bed and approached the door. As I did so there came faintly from the next room the unmistakable sound of someone retreating stealthily across the floor. Yet, as I heard it, it was neither the tread of a man nor a regular footstep, but rather, it seemed to me, a confused sort of crawling, almost as of someone on his hands and knees.

I unlocked the door in less than a second, and passed quickly into the front room, and I could feel, as by the subtlest imaginable vibrations upon my nerves, that the spot I was standing in had just that instant been vacated! The Listener had moved; he was now behind the other door, standing in the passage. Yet this door was also closed. I moved swiftly, and as silently as possible, across the floor, and turned the handle. A cold rush of air met me from the passage and sent shiver after shiver down my back. There was no one in the doorway; there was no one on the little landing; there was no one moving down the staircase. Yet I had been so quick that this midnight Listener could not be very far away, and I felt that if I persevered I should eventually come face to face with him. And the courage that came so opportunely to overcome my nervousness and horror seemed born of the unwilling conviction that it was somehow necessary for my safety as well as my sanity that I should find this intruder and force his secret from him. For was it not the intent action of his mind upon my own, in concentrated listening, that had awakened me with such a vivid realization of his presence?

Advancing across the narrow landing, I peered down into the well of the little house. There was nothing to be seen; no one was moving in the darkness. How cold the oilcloth was to my bare feet.

I cannot say what it was that suddenly drew my eyes upward. I only know that, without apparent reason, I looked up and saw a person about half-way up the next turn of the stairs, leaning forward over the balustrade and staring straight into my face. It was a man. He appeared to be clinging to the rail rather than standing on the stairs. The gloom made it impossible to see much beyond the general outline, but the head and shoulders were seemingly enormous, and stood sharply silhouetted against the skylight in the roof immediately above. The idea flashed into my brain in a moment that I was looking into the visage of something monstrous. The huge skull, the mane-like hair, the wide-humped shoulders, suggested, in a way I did not pause to analyze, that which was scarcely human; and for some seconds, fascinated by horror, I returned the gaze and stared into the dark, inscrutable countenance above me, without knowing exactly where I was or what I was doing. Then I realized in quite a new way that I was face to face with the secret midnight Listener, and I steeled myself as best I could for what was about to come.

The source of the rash courage that came to me at this awful moment will ever be to me an inexplicable mystery. Though shivering with fear, and my forehead wet with an unholy dew, I resolved to advance. Twenty questions leaped to my lips: What are you? What do you want? Why do you listen and watch? Why do you come into my room? But none of them found articulate utterance.

I began forthwith to climb the stairs, and with the first signs of my advance *he* drew himself back into the shadows and began to move too. He retreated as swiftly as I advanced. I heard the sound of his crawling motion a few steps ahead of me, ever maintaining the same distance. When I reached the landing he was half-way up the next flight, and when I was half-way up the next flight he had already arrived at the top landing. And then I heard him open the door of the little square room under the roof and go in. Immediately, though the door did not close after him, the sound of his moving entirely ceased.

At this moment I longed for a light, or a stick, or any weapon whatsoever; but I had none of these things, and it was impossible to go back. So I marched steadily up the rest of the stairs, and in less than a minute found myself standing in the gloom face to face with the door through which this creature had just entered.

For a moment I hesitated. The door was about half-way open, and the Listener was standing evidently in his favourite attitude just behind it – listening. To search through that dark room for him seemed hopeless; to enter the same small space where he was seemed horrible. The very idea filled me with loathing, and I almost decided to turn back.

It is strange at such times how trivial things impinge on the consciousness with a shock as of something important and immense. Something – it might have been a beetle or a mouse – scuttled over the bare boards behind me. The door moved a quarter of an inch, closing. My decision came back with a sudden rush, as it were, and thrusting out a foot, I kicked the door so that it swung sharply back to its full extent, and permitted me to walk forward slowly into the aperture of profound blackness beyond. What a queer soft sound my bare feet made on the boards! How the blood sang and buzzed in my head!

I was inside. The darkness closed over me, hiding even the windows. I groped my way round the walls in a thorough search; but in order to prevent all possibility of the other's escape, I first of all *closed the door*.

There we were, we two, shut in together between

four walls, within a few feet of one another. But with what, with whom, was I thus momentarily imprisoned? A new light flashed suddenly over the affair with a swift, illuminating brilliance — and I knew I was a fool, an utter fool! I was wide awake at last, and the horror was evaporating. My cursed nerves again; a dream, a nightmare, and the old result — walking in my sleep. The figure was a dream-figure. Many a time before had the actors in my dreams stood before me for some moments after I was awake.... There was a chance match in my pajamas' pocket, and I struck it on the wall. The room was utterly empty. It held not even a shadow. I went quickly down to bed, cursing my wretched nerves and my foolish, vivid dreams. But as soon as ever I was asleep again, the same uncouth figure of a man crept back to my bedside, and bending over me with his immense head close to my ear whispered repeatedly in my dreams, "I want your body; I want its covering. I'm waiting for it, and listening always." Words scarcely less foolish than the dream.

But I wonder what that queer odour was up in the square room. I noticed it again, and stronger than ever before and it seemed to be also in my bedroom when I woke this morning.

*****

Nov. 29. — Slowly, as moonbeams rise over a misty sea in June, the thought is entering my mind that my nerves and somnambulistic dreams do not adequately account for the influence this house exercises upon me. It holds me as with a fine, invisible net. I cannot escape if I would. It draws me, and it means to keep me.

*****

Nov. 30. — The post this morning brought me a letter from Aden, forwarded from my old rooms in Earl's Court. It was from Chapter, my former Trinity chum, who is on his way home from the East, and asks for my address. I sent it to him at the hotel he mentioned, "to await arrival."

As I have already said, my windows command a view of the alley, and I can see an arrival without difficulty. This morning, while I was busy writing, the sound of footsteps coming up the alley filled me with a sense of vague alarm that I could in no way account for. I went over to the window, and saw a man standing below waiting for the door to be opened. His shoulders were broad, his top-hat glossy, and his overcoat fitted beautifully round the collar. All this I could see, but no more. Presently the door opened, and the shock to my nerves was unmistakable when I heard a man's voice ask, "Is Mr. — — still here?" mentioning my name. I could not catch the answer, but it could only have been in the affirmative, for the man entered the hall and the door shut to behind him. But I waited in vain for the sound of his steps on the stairs. There was no sound of any kind. It seemed to me so strange that I opened my door and looked out. No one was anywhere to be seen. I walked across the narrow landing, and looked through the window that commands the whole length of the alley. There was no sign of a human being, coming or going. The lane was deserted. Then I deliberately walked downstairs into the kitchen, and asked the gray-faced landlady if a gentleman had just that minute called for me.

The answer, given with an odd, weary sort of smile, was "No!"

*****

Dec. 1. — I feel genuinely alarmed and uneasy over the state of my nerves. Dreams are dreams, but never before have I had dreams in broad daylight.

I am looking forward very much to Chapter's arrival. He is a capital fellow, vigorous, healthy, with no nerves, and even less imagination; and he has £2000 a year into the bargain. Periodically he makes me offers — the last was to travel round the world with him as secretary, which was a delicate way of paying my expenses and giving me some pocket-money — offers, however, which I invariably decline. I prefer to keep his friendship. Women could not come between us; money might — therefore I give it no opportunity. Chapter always laughed at what he called my "fancies," being himself possessed only of that thin-blooded quality of imagination which is ever associated with the prosaic-minded man. Yet, if taunted with this obvious lack, his wrath is deeply stirred. His psychology is that of the crass materialist — always a rather funny article. It will afford me genuine relief, none the less, to hear the cold judgment his mind will have to pass upon the story of this house as I shall have it to tell.

*****

Dec. 2. — The strangest part of it all I have not referred to in this brief diary. Truth to tell, I have been afraid to set it down in black and white. I have kept it in the background of my thoughts, preventing it as far as possible from taking shape. In spite of my efforts, however, it has continued to grow stronger.

Now that I come to face the issue squarely, it is harder to express than I imagined. Like a half-remembered melody that trips in the head but vanishes the moment you try to sing it, these thoughts form a group in the background of my mind, *behind* my mind, as it were, and refuse to come forward. They are crouching ready to spring, but the actual leap never takes place.

In these rooms, except when my mind is strongly concentrated on my own work, I find myself suddenly dealing in thoughts and ideas that are not my own! New, strange conceptions, wholly foreign to my temperament, are forever cropping up in my head. What precisely they are is of no particular importance. The point is that they are entirely apart from the channel in which my thoughts have hitherto been accustomed to flow. Especially they come when my mind is at rest, unoccupied; when I'm dreaming over the fire, or sitting with a book which fails to hold my attention. Then these thoughts which are not mine spring into life and make me feel exceedingly uncomfortable. Sometimes they are so strong that I almost feel as if someone were in the room beside me, thinking aloud.

Evidently my nerves and liver are shockingly out of order. I must work harder and take more vigorous exercise. The horrid thoughts never come when my mind is much occupied. But they are always there — waiting and as it were *alive*.

What I have attempted to describe above came first upon me gradually after I had been some days in the house, and then grew steadily in strength. The other strange thing has come to me only twice in all these weeks. *It appals me.* It is the consciousness of the propinquity of some deadly and loathsome disease. It comes over me like a wave of fever heat, and then passes off, leaving me cold and trembling. The air seems for a few seconds to become tainted. So penetrating and convincing is the thought of this sickness, that on both occasions my brain has turned momentarily dizzy, and through my mind, like flames of white heat, have flashed the ominous names of all the dangerous illnesses I know. I can no more explain these visitations than I can fly, yet I know there is no dreaming about the clammy skin and palpitating heart which they always leave as witnesses of their brief visit.

Most strongly of all was I aware of this nearness of a mortal sickness when, on the night of the 28th, I went upstairs in pursuit of the listening figure. When we were shut in together in that little square room under the roof, I felt that I was face to face with the actual essence of this invisible and malignant disease. Such a feeling never entered my heart before, and I pray to God it never may again.

There! Now I have confessed. I have given some expression at least to the feelings that so far I have been afraid to see in my own writing. For — since I can no longer deceive myself — the experiences of that night (28th) were no more a dream than my daily breakfast is a dream; and the trivial entry in this diary by which I sought to explain away an occurrence that caused me unutterable horror was due solely to my desire not to acknowledge in words what I really felt and believed to be true. The increase that would have accrued to my horror by so doing might have been more than I could stand.

*****

Dec. 3. — I wish Chapter would come. My facts are all ready marshalled, and I can see his cool, gray eyes fixed incredulously on my face as I relate them: the knocking at my door, the well-dressed caller, the light in the upper window and the shadow upon the blind, the man who preceded me in the snow, the scattering of my clothes at night, Emily's arrested confession, the landlady's suspicious reticence, the midnight listener on the stairs, and those awful subsequent words in my sleep; and above all, and hardest to tell, the presence of the abominable sickness, and the stream of thoughts and ideas that are not my own.

I can see Chapter's face, and I can almost hear his deliberate words, "You've been at the tea again, and underfeeding, I expect, as usual. Better see my nerve doctor, and then come with me to the south of France." For this fellow, who knows nothing of disordered liver or high-strung nerves, goes regularly to a great nerve specialist with the periodical belief that his nervous system is beginning to decay.

*****

Dec. 5. — Ever since the incident of the Listener, I have kept a night-light burning in my bedroom, and my sleep has been undisturbed. Last night, however, I was subjected to a far worse annoyance. I woke suddenly, and saw a man in front of the dressing-table regarding himself in the mirror. The door was locked, as usual. I knew at once it was the Listener, and the blood turned to ice in my veins. Such a wave of horror and dread swept over me that it seemed to turn me rigid in the bed, and I could neither move nor speak. I noted, however, that the odour I so abhorred was strong in the room.

The man seemed to be tall and broad. He was stooping forward over the mirror. His back was turned to me, but in the glass I saw the reflection of a huge head and face illumined fitfully by the flicker of the night-light. The spectral gray of very early morning stealing in round the edges of the curtains lent an additional horror to the picture, for it fell upon the hair that was tawny and mane-like, hanging about a face whose swollen, rugose features bore the once seen never forgotten leonine expression of — I dare not write down that awful word. But, by way of corroborative proof, I saw in the faint mingling of the two lights that there were several bronze-coloured blotches on the cheeks which the man was evidently examining with great care in the glass. The lips were pale and very thick and large. One hand I could not see, but the other rested on the ivory back of my hairbrush. Its muscles were strangely contracted, the fingers thin to emaciation, the back of the hand closely puckered up. It was like a big gray spider crouching to spring, or the claw of a great bird.

The full realization that I was alone in the room with this nameless creature, almost within arm's reach of him, overcame me to such a degree that, when he suddenly turned and regarded me with small beady eyes, wholly out of proportion to the grandeur of their massive setting, I sat bolt upright in bed, uttered a loud cry, and then fell back in a dead swoon of terror upon the bed.

*****

Dec. 6. — ... When I came to this morning, the first thing I noticed was that my clothes were strewn all over the floor.... I find it difficult to put my thoughts together, and have sudden accesses of violent trembling. I determined that I would go at once to Chapter's hotel and find out when he is expected. I cannot refer to what happened in the night; it is too awful, and I have to keep my thoughts rigorously away from it. I feel lightheaded and queer, couldn't eat any breakfast, and have twice vomited with blood. While dressing to go out, a hansom rattled up noisily over the cobbles, and a minute later the door opened, and to my great joy in walked the very subject of my thoughts.

The sight of his strong face and quiet eyes had an immediate effect upon me, and I grew calmer again. His very handshake was a sort of tonic. But, as I listened eagerly to the deep tones of his reassuring voice, and the visions of the night time paled a little, I began to realize how very hard it was going to be to tell him my wild, intangible tale. Some men radiate an animal vigour that destroys the delicate woof of a vision and effectually prevents its reconstruction. Chapter was one of these men.

We talked of incidents that had filled the interval since we last met, and he told me something of his travels. He talked and I listened. But, so full was I of the horrid thing I had to tell that I made a poor listener. I was forever watching my opportunity to leap in and explode it all under his nose.

Before very long, however, it was borne in upon me that he too was merely talking for time. He too held something of importance in the background of his mind, something too weighty to let fall till the right moment presented itself. So that during the whole of the first half-hour we were both waiting for the psychological moment in which properly to release our respective bombs; and the intensity of our minds' action set up opposing forces that merely sufficed to hold one another in check – and nothing more. As soon as I realized this, therefore, I resolved to yield. I renounced for the time my purpose of telling my story, and had the satisfaction of seeing that his mind, released from the restraint of my own, at once began to make preparations for the discharge of its momentous burden. The talk grew less and less magnetic; the interest waned; the descriptions of his travels became less alive. There were pauses between his sentences. Presently he repeated himself. His words clothed no living thoughts. The pauses grew longer. Then the interest dwindled altogether and went out like a candle in the wind. His voice ceased, and he looked up squarely into my face with serious and anxious eyes.

The psychological moment had come at last!

"I say — " he began, and then stopped short.

I made an unconscious gesture of encouragement, but said no word. I dreaded the impending disclosure exceedingly. A dark shadow seemed to precede it.

"I say," he blurted out at last, "what in the world made you ever come to this place — to these rooms, I mean?"

"They're cheap, for one thing," I began, "and central and — "

"They're too cheap," he interrupted. "Didn't you ask what made 'em so cheap?"

"It never occurred to me at the time."

There was a pause in which he avoided my eyes.

"For God's sake, go on, man, and tell it!" I cried, for the suspense was getting more than I could stand in my nervous condition.

"This was where Blount lived so long," he said quietly, "and where he — died. You know, in the old days I often used to come here and see him and do what I could to alleviate his — " He stuck fast again.

"Well!" I said with a great effort. "*Please* go on — faster."

"But," Chapter went on, turning his face to the window with a perceptible shiver, "he finally got so terrible I simply couldn't stand it, though I always thought I could stand anything. It got on my nerves and made me dream, and haunted me day and night."

I stared at him, and said nothing. I had never heard of Blount in my life, and didn't know what he was talking about. But all the same, I was trembling, and my mouth had become strangely dry.

"This is the first time I've been back here since," he said almost in a whisper, "and, 'pon my word, it gives me the creeps. I swear it isn't fit for a man to live in. I never saw you look so bad, old man."

"I've got it for a year," I jerked out, with a forced laugh; "signed the lease and all. I thought it was rather a bargain."

Chapter shuddered, and buttoned his overcoat up to his neck. Then he spoke in a low voice, looking occasionally behind him as though he thought someone was listening. I too could have sworn someone else was in the room with us.

"He did it himself, you know, and no one blamed him a bit; his sufferings were awful. For the last two years he used to wear a veil when he went out, and even then it was always in a closed carriage. Even the attendant who had nursed him for so long was at length obliged to leave. The extremities of both the lower limbs were gone, dropped off, and he moved about the ground on all fours with a sort of crawling motion. The odour, too, was — "

I was obliged to interrupt him here. I could hear no more details of that sort. My skin was moist, I felt hot and cold by turns, for at last I was beginning to understand.

"Poor devil," Chapter went on; "I used to keep my eyes closed as much as possible. He always begged to be allowed to take his veil off, and asked if I minded very much. I used to stand by the open window. He never touched me, though. He rented the whole house. Nothing would induce him to leave it."

"Did he occupy — these very rooms?"

"No. He had the little room on the top floor, the square one just under the roof. He preferred it because it was dark. These rooms were too near the ground, and he was afraid people might see him through the windows. A crowd had been known to follow him up to the very door, and then stand below the windows in the hope of catching a glimpse of his face."

"But there were hospitals."

"He wouldn't go near one, and they didn't like to force him. You know, they say it's *not* contagious, so there was nothing to prevent his staying here if he wanted to. He spent all his time reading medical books, about drugs and so on. His head and face were something appalling, just like a lion's."

I held up my hand to arrest further description.

"He was a burden to the world, and he knew it. One night I suppose he realized it too keenly to wish to live. He had the free use of drugs — and in the morning he was found dead on the floor. Two years ago, that was, and they said then he had still several years to live."

"Then, in Heaven's name!" I cried, unable to bear the suspense any longer, "tell me what it was he had, and be quick about it."

"I thought you knew!" he exclaimed, with genuine surprise. "I thought you knew!"

He leaned forward and our eyes met. In a scarcely audible whisper I caught the words his lip seemed almost afraid to utter:

"He was a leper!"

II. Number 13 — Montague Rhodes James

Among the towns of Jutland, Viborg justly holds a high place. It is the seat of a bishopric; it has a handsome but almost entirely new cathedral, a charming garden, a lake of great beauty, and many storks. Near it is Hald, accounted one of the prettiest things in Denmark, and hard by is Finderup, where Marsk Stig murdered King Erik Glipping on St. Cecilia's Day, in the year 1286. Fifty-six blows of square-headed iron maces were traced on Erik's skull when his tomb was opened in the seventeenth century. But I am not writing a guide-book.

There are good hotels in Viborg — Preisler's and the Phœnix are all that can be desired. But my cousin whose experiences I have to tell you now, went to the Golden Lion the first time that he visited Viborg. He has not been there since, and the following pages will perhaps explain the reason of his abstention.

The Golden Lion is one of the very few houses in the town that were not destroyed in the great fire of 1726, which practically demolished the cathedral, the Sognekirke, the Raadhuus, and so much else that was old and interesting. It is a great red-brick house — that is, the front is of brick, with corbie steps on the gables and a text over the door, but the courtyard into which the omnibus drives is of black and white wood and plaster.

The sun was declining in the heavens when my cousin walked up to the door, and the light smote full upon the imposing façade of the house. He was delighted with the old-fashioned aspect of the place, and promised himself a thoroughly satisfactory and amusing stay in an inn so typical of old Jutland.

It was not business in the ordinary sense of the word that had brought Mr. Anderson to Viborg. He was engaged upon some researches into the Church history of Denmark, and it had come to his knowledge that in the Rigsarkiv of Viborg there were papers, saved from the fire, relating to the last days of Roman Catholicism in the country. He proposed, therefore, to spend a considerable time — perhaps as much as a fortnight or three weeks — in examining and copying these, and he hoped that the Golden Lion would be able to give him a room of sufficient size to serve alike as a bedroom and a study. His wishes were explained to the landlord, and, after a certain amount of thought, the latter suggested that perhaps it might be the best way for the gentleman to look at one or two of the larger rooms and pick one for himself. It seemed a good idea.

The top floor was soon rejected as entailing too much getting upstairs after the day's work; the second floor contained no room of exactly the dimensions required; but on the first floor there was a choice of two or three rooms which would, so far as size went, suit admirably.

The landlord was strongly in favour of Number 17, but Mr. Anderson pointed out that its windows commanded only the blank wall of the next house, and that it would be very dark in the afternoon. Either Number 12 or Number 14 would be better, for both of them looked on the street, and the bright evening light and the pretty view would more than compensate him for the additional amount of noise.

Eventually Number 12 was selected. Like its neighbours, it had three windows, all on one side of the room; it was fairly high and unusually long. There was, of course, no fireplace, but the stove was handsome and rather old — a cast-iron erection, on the side of which was a representation of Abraham sacrificing Isaac, and the inscription, "1 Bog Mose, Cap. 22," above. Nothing else in the room was remarkable; the only interesting picture was an old coloured print of the town, date about 1820.

Supper-time was approaching, but when Anderson, refreshed by the ordinary ablutions, descended the staircase, there were still a few minutes before the bell rang. He devoted them to examining the list of his fellow-lodgers. As is usual in Denmark, their names were displayed on a large blackboard, divided into columns and lines, the numbers of the rooms being painted in at the beginning of each line. The list was not exciting. There was an advocate, or Sagförer, a German, and some bagmen from Copenhagen. The one and only point which suggested any food for thought was the absence of any Number 13 from the tale of the rooms, and even this was a thing which Anderson had already noticed half a dozen times in his experience of Danish hotels. He could not help wondering whether the objection to that particular number, common as it is, was so widespread and so strong as to make it difficult to let a room so ticketed, and he resolved to ask the landlord if he and his colleagues in the profession had actually met with many clients who refused to be accommodated in the thirteenth room.

He had nothing to tell me (I am giving the story as I heard it from him) about what passed at supper, and the evening, which was spent in unpacking and arranging his clothes, books, and papers, was not more eventful. Toward eleven o'clock he resolved to go to bed, but with him, as with a good many other people nowadays, an almost necessary preliminary to bed, if he meant to sleep, was the reading of a few pages of print, and he now remembered that the particular book which he had been reading in the train, and which alone would satisfy him at that present moment, was in the pocket of his greatcoat, then hanging on a peg outside the dining-room.

To run down and secure it was the work of a moment, and, as the passages were by no means dark, it was not difficult for him to find his way back to his own door. So, at least, he thought; but when he arrived there, and turned the handle, the door entirely refused to open, and he caught the sound of a hasty movement toward it from within. He had tried the wrong door, of course. Was his own room to the right or to the left? He glanced at the number: it was 13. His room would be on the left; and so it was. And not before he had been in bed for some minutes, had read his wonted three or four pages of his book, blown out his light, and turned over to go to sleep, did it occur to him that, whereas on the blackboard of the hotel there had been no Number 13, there was undoubtedly a room numbered 13 in the hotel. He felt rather sorry he had not chosen it for his own. Perhaps he might have done the landlord a little service by occupying it, and given him the chance of saying that a well-worn English gentleman had lived in it for three weeks and liked it very much. But probably it was used as a servant's room or something of the kind. After all, it was most likely not so large or good a room as his own. And he looked drowsily about the room, which was fairly perceptible in the half-light from the streetlamp. It was a curious effect, he thought. Rooms usually look larger in a dim light than a full one, but this seemed to have contracted in length and grown proportionately higher. Well, well! sleep was more important than these vague ruminations — and to sleep he went.

On the day after his arrival Anderson attacked the Rigsarkiv of Viborg. He was, as one might expect in Denmark, kindly received, and access to all that he wished to see was made as easy for him as possible. The documents laid before him were far more numerous and interesting than he had at all anticipated. Besides official papers, there was a large bundle of correspondence relating to Bishop Jörgen Friis, the last Roman Catholic who held the see, and in these there cropped up many amusing and what are called "intimate" details of private life and individual character. There was much talk of a house owned by the Bishop, but not inhabited by him in the town. Its tenant was apparently somewhat of a scandal and a stumbling-block to the reforming party. He was a disgrace, they wrote, to the city; he practised secret and wicked arts, and had sold his soul to the enemy. It was of a piece with the gross corruption and superstition of the Babylonish Church that such a viper and blood-sucking *Troldmand* should be patronized and harboured by the Bishop. The Bishop met these reproaches boldly; he protested his own abhorrence of all such things as secret arts, and required his antagonists to bring the matter before the proper court — of course, the spiritual court — and sift it to the bottom. No one could be more ready and willing than himself to condemn Mag. Nicolas Francken if the evidence showed him to have been guilty of any of the crimes informally alleged against him.

Anderson had not time to do more than glance at the next letter of the Protestant leader, Rasmus Nielsen, before the record office was closed for the day, but he gathered its general tenor, which was to the effect that Christian men were now no longer bound by the decisions of Bishops of Rome, and that the Bishop's Court was not, and could not be, a fit or competent tribunal to judge so grave and weighty a cause.

On leaving the office, Mr. Anderson was accompanied by the old gentleman who presided over it, and, as they walked, the conversation very naturally turned to the papers of which I have just been speaking.

Herr Scavenius, the Archivist of Viborg, though very well informed as to the general run of the documents under his charge, was not a specialist in those of the Reformation period. He was much interested in what Anderson had to tell him about them. He looked forward with great pleasure, he said, to seeing the publication in which Mr. Anderson spoke of embodying their contents. "This house of the Bishop Friis," he added, "it is a great puzzle to me where it can have stood. I have studied carefully the topography of old Viborg, but it is most unlucky – of the old terrier of the Bishop's property which was made in 1560, and of which we have the greater part in the Arkiv, just the piece which had the list of the town property is missing. Never mind. Perhaps I shall some day succeed to find him."

After taking some exercise – I forget exactly how or where – Anderson went back to the Golden Lion, his supper, his game of patience, and his bed. On the way to his room it occurred to him that he had forgotten to talk to the landlord about the omission of Number 13 from the hotel board, and also that he might as well make sure that Number 13 did actually exist before he made any reference to the matter.

The decision was not difficult to arrive at. There

was the door with its number as plain as could be, and work of some kind was evidently going on inside it, for as he neared the door he could hear footsteps and voices, or a voice, within. During the few seconds in which he halted to make sure of the number, the footsteps ceased, seemingly very near the door, and he was a little startled at hearing a quick hissing breathing as of a person in strong excitement. He went on to his own room, and again he was surprised to find how much smaller it seemed now than it had when he selected it. It was a slight disappointment, but only slight. If he found it really not large enough, he could very easily shift to another. In the meantime he wanted something — as far as I remember it was a pocket-handkerchief — out of his portmanteau, which had been placed by the porter on a very inadequate trestle or stool against the wall at the furthest end of the room from his bed. Here was a very curious thing: the portmanteau was not to be seen. It had been moved by officious servants; doubtless the contents had been put in the wardrobe. No, none of them were there. This was vexatious. The idea of a theft he dismissed at once. Such things rarely happen in Denmark, but some piece of stupidity had certainly been performed (which is not so uncommon), and the *stuepige* must be severely spoken to. Whatever it was that he wanted, it was not so necessary to his comfort that he could not wait till the morning for it, and he therefore settled not to ring the bell and disturb the servants. He went to the window — the right-hand window it was — and looked out on the quiet street. There was a tall building opposite, with large spaces of dead wall; no passers by; a dark night; and very little to be seen of any kind.

The light was behind him, and he could see his own shadow clearly cast on the wall opposite. Also the shadow of the bearded man in Number 11 on the left, who passed to and fro in shirt sleeves once or twice, and was seen first brushing his hair, and later on in a nightgown. Also the shadow of the occupant of Number 13 on the right. This might be more interesting. Number 13 was, like himself, leaning on his elbows on the window-sill looking out into the street. He seemed to be a tall thin man — or was it by any chance a woman? — at least, it was someone who covered his or her head with some kind of drapery before going to bed, and, he thought, must be possessed of a red lamp-shade — and the lamp must be flickering very much. There was a distinct playing up and down of a dull red light on the opposite wall. He craned out a little to see if he could make any more of the figure, but beyond a fold of some light, perhaps white, material on the window-sill he could see nothing.

Now came a distant step in the street, and its approach seemed to recall Number 13 to a sense of his exposed position, for very swiftly and suddenly he swept aside from the window, and his red light went out. Anderson, who had been smoking a cigarette, laid the end of it on the window-sill and went to bed.

Next morning he was woke by the *stuepige* with hot water, etc. He roused himself, and after thinking out the correct Danish words, said as distinctly as he could:

"You must not move my portmanteau. Where is it?"

As is not uncommon, the maid laughed, and went away without making any distinct answer.

Anderson, rather irritated, sat up in bed, intending to call her back, but he remained sitting up, staring straight in front of him. There was his portmanteau on its trestle, exactly where he had seen the porter put it when he first arrived. This was a rude shock for a man who prided himself on his accuracy of observation. How it could possibly have escaped him the night before he did not pretend to understand; at any rate, there it was now.

The daylight showed more than the portmanteau; it let the true proportions of the room with its three windows appear, and satisfied its tenant that his choice after all had not been a bad one. When he was almost dressed he walked to the middle one of the three windows to look out at the weather. Another shock awaited him. Strangely unobservant he must have been last night. He could have sworn ten times over that he had been smoking at the right-hand window the last thing before he went to bed, and here was his cigarette-end on the sill of the middle window.

He started to go down to breakfast. Rather late, but Number 13 was later: here were his boots still outside his door – a gentleman's boots. So then Number 13 was a man, not a woman. Just then he caught sight of the number on the door. It was 14. He thought he must have passed Number 13 without noticing it. Three stupid mistakes in twelve hours were too much for a methodical, accurate-minded man, so he turned back to make sure. The next number to 14 was number 12, his own room. There was no Number 13 at all.

After some minutes devoted to a careful consideration of everything he had had to eat and drink during the last twenty-four hours, Anderson decided to give the question up. If his eyes or his brain were giving way he would have plenty of opportunities for ascertaining that fact; if not, then he was evidently being treated to a very interesting experience. In either case the development of events would certainly be worth watching.

During the day he continued his examination of the episcopal correspondence which I have already summarized. To his disappointment, it was incomplete. Only one other letter could be found which referred to the affair of Mag. Nicolas Francken. It was from the Bishop Jörgen Friis to Rasmus Nielsen. He said:

"Although we are not in the least degree inclined to assent to your judgment concerning our court, and shall be prepared if need be to withstand you to the uttermost in that behalf, yet forasmuch as our trusty and well-beloved Mag. Nicolas Francken, against whom you have dared to allege certain false and malicious charges, hath been suddenly removed from among us, it is apparent that the question for this term falls. But forasmuch as you further allege that the Apostle and Evangelist St. John in his heavenly Apocalypse describes the Holy Roman Church under the guise and symbol of the Scarlet Woman, be it known to you," etc.

Search as he would, Anderson could find no sequel to this letter nor any clue to the cause or manner of the "removal" of the *casus belli*. He could only suppose that Francken had died suddenly; and as there were only two days between the date of Nielsen's last letter — when Francken was evidently still in being — and that of the Bishop's letter, the death must have been completely unexpected.

In the afternoon he paid a short visit to Hald, and took his tea at Baekkelund; nor could he notice, though he was in a somewhat nervous frame of mind, that there was any indication of such a failure of eye or brain as his experiences of the morning had led him to fear.

At supper he found himself next to the landlord.

"What," he asked him, after some indifferent conversation, "is the reason why in most of the hotels one visits in this country the number thirteen is left out of the list of rooms? I see you have none here."

The landlord seemed amused.

"To think that you should have noticed a thing like that! I've thought about it once or twice, myself, to tell the truth. An educated man, I've said, has no business with these superstitious notions. I was brought up myself here in the high school of Viborg, and our old master was always a man to set his face against anything of that kind. He's been dead now this many years — a fine upstanding man he was, and ready with his hands as well as his head. I recollect us boys, one snowy day — "

Here he plunged into reminiscence.

"Then you don't think there is any particular objection to having a Number 13?" said Anderson.

"Ah! to be sure. Well, you understand, I was brought up to the business by my poor old father. He kept an hotel in Aarhuus first, and then, when we were born, he moved to Viborg here, which was his native place, and had the Phœnix here until he died. That was in 1876. Then I started business in Silkeborg, and only the year before last I moved into this house."

Then followed more details as to the state of the house and business when first taken over.

"And when you came here, was there a Number 13?"

"No, no. I was going to tell you about that. You see, in a place like this, the commercial class — the travellers — are what we have to provide for in general. And put them in Number 13? Why, they'd as soon sleep in the street, or sooner. As far as I'm concerned myself, it wouldn't make a penny difference to me what the number of my room was, and so I've often said to them; but they stick to it that it brings them bad luck. Quantities of stories they have among them of men that have slept in a Number 13 and never been the same again, or lost their best customers, or — one thing and another," said the landlord, after searching for a more graphic phrase.

"Then, what do you use your Number 13 for?" said Anderson, conscious as he said the words of a curious anxiety quite disproportionate to the importance of the question.

"My Number 13? Why, don't I tell you that there isn't such a thing in the house? I thought you might have noticed that. If there was it would be next door to your own room."

"Well, yes; only I happened to think — that is, I fancied last night that I had seen a door numbered thirteen in that passage; and, really, I am almost certain I must have been right, for I saw it the night before as well."

Of course, Herr Kristensen laughed this notion to scorn, as Anderson had expected, and emphasized with much iteration the fact that no Number 13 existed or had existed before him in that hotel.

Anderson was in some ways relieved by his certainty, but still puzzled, and he began to think that the best way to make sure whether he had indeed been subject to an illusion or not was to invite the landlord to his room to smoke a cigar later on in the evening. Some photographs of English towns which he had with him formed a sufficiently good excuse.

Herr Kristensen was flattered by the invitation, and most willingly accepted it. At about ten o'clock he was to make his appearance, but before that Anderson had some letters to write, and retired for the purpose of writing them. He almost blushed to himself at confessing it, but he could not deny that it was the fact that he was becoming quite nervous about the question of the existence of Number 13; so much so that he approached his room by way of Number 11, in order that he might not be obliged to pass the door, or the place where the door ought to be. He looked quickly and suspiciously about the room when he entered it, but there was nothing beyond that indefinable air of being smaller than usual, to warrant any misgivings. There was no question of the presence or absence of his portmanteau to-night. He had himself emptied it of its contents and lodged it under his bed. With a certain effort he dismissed the thought of Number 13 from his mind, and sat down to his writing.

His neighbours were quiet enough. Occasionally a door opened in the passage and a pair of boots was thrown out, or a bagman walked past humming to himself, and outside, from time to time a cart thundered over the atrocious cobble-stones, or a quick step hurried along the flags.

Anderson finished his letters, ordered in whiskey and soda, and then went to the window and studied the dead wall opposite and the shadows upon it.

As far as he could remember, Number 14 had been occupied by the lawyer, a staid man, who said little at meals, being generally engaged in studying a small bundle of papers beside his plate. Apparently, however, he was in the habit of giving vent to his animal spirits when alone. Why else should he be dancing? The shadow from the next room evidently showed that he was. Again and again his thin form crossed the window, his arms waved, and a gaunt leg was kicked up with surprising agility. He seemed to be barefooted, and the floor must be well laid, for no sound betrayed his movements. Sagförer Herr Anders Jensen, dancing at ten o'clock at night in a hotel bedroom, seemed a fitting subject for a historical painting in the grand style; and Anderson's thoughts, like those of Emily in the "Mysteries of Udolpho," began to "arrange themselves in the following lines":

"When I return to my hotel,
At ten o'clock P.M.,
The waiters think I am unwell;
I do not care for them.
But when I've locked my chamber door,
And put my boots outside,
I dance all night upon the floor.
And even if my neighbours swore,
I'd go on dancing all the more,
For I'm acquainted with the law,
And in despite of all their jaw,
Their protests I deride."

Had not the landlord at this moment knocked at the door, it is probable that quite a long poem might have been laid before the reader. To judge from his look of surprise when he found himself in the room, Herr Kristensen was struck, as Anderson had been, by something unusual in its aspect. But he made no remark. Anderson's photographs interested him mightily, and formed the text of many autobiographical discourses. Nor is it quite clear how the conversation could have been diverted into the desired channel of Number 13, had not the lawyer at this moment begun to sing, and to sing in a manner which could leave no doubt in anyone's mind that he was either exceedingly drunk or raving mad. It was a high, thin voice that they heard, and it seemed dry, as if from long disuse. Of words or tune there was no question. It went sailing up to a surprising height, and was carried down with a despairing moan as of a winter wind in a hollow chimney, or an organ whose wind fails suddenly. It was a really horrible sound, and Anderson felt that if he had been alone he must have fled for refuge and society to some neighbour bagman's room.

The landlord sat open-mouthed.

"I don't understand it," he said at last, wiping his forehead. "It is dreadful. I have heard it once before, but I made sure it was a cat."

"Is he mad?" said Anderson.

"He must be; and what a sad thing! Such a good customer, too, and so successful in his business, by what I hear, and a young family to bring up."

Just then came an impatient knock at the door, and the knocker entered, without waiting to be asked. It was the lawyer, in deshabille and very rough-haired; and very angry he looked.

"I beg pardon, sir," he said, "but I should be much obliged if you would kindly desist — "

Here he stopped, for it was evident that neither of the persons before him was responsible for the disturbance; and after a moment's lull it swelled forth again more wildly than before.

"But what in the name of Heaven does it mean?" broke out the lawyer. "Where is it? Who is it? Am I going out of my mind?"

"Surely, Herr Jensen, it comes from your room next door? Isn't there a cat or something stuck in the chimney?"

This was the best that occurred to Anderson to say, and he realized its futility as he spoke; but any thing was better than to stand and listen to that horrible voice, and look at the broad, white face of the landlord, all perspiring and quivering as he clutched the arms of his chair.

"Impossible," said the lawyer, "impossible. There is no chimney. I came here because I was convinced the noise was going on here. It was certainly in the next room to mine."

"Was there no door between yours and mine?" said Anderson eagerly.

"No, sir," said Herr Jensen, rather sharply. "At least, not this morning."

"Ah!" said Anderson. "Nor to-night?"

"I am not sure," said the lawyer with some hesitation.

Suddenly the crying or singing voice in the next room died away, and the singer was heard seemingly to laugh to himself in a crooning manner. The three men actually shivered at the sound. Then there was a silence.

"Come," said the lawyer, "what have you to say,

Herr Kristensen? What does this mean?"

"Good Heaven!" said Kristensen. "How should I tell! I know no more than you, gentlemen. I pray I may never hear such a noise again."

"So do I," said Herr Jensen, and he added something under his breath. Anderson thought it sounded like the last words of the Psalter, "*omnis spiritus laudet Dominum,*" but he could not be sure.

"But we must do something," said Anderson – "the three of us. Shall we go and investigate in the next room?"

"But that is Herr Jensen's room," wailed the landlord. "It is no use; he has come from there himself."

"I am not so sure," said Jensen. "I think this gentleman is right: we must go and see."

The only weapons of defence that could be mustered on the spot were a stick and umbrella. The expedition went out into the passage, not without quakings. There was a deadly quiet outside, but a light shone from under the next door. Anderson and Jensen approached it. The latter turned the handle, and gave a sudden vigorous push. No use. The door stood fast.

"Herr Kristensen," said Jensen, "will you go and fetch the strongest servant you have in the place? We must see this through."

The landlord nodded, and hurried off, glad to be away from the scene of action. Jensen and Anderson remained outside looking at the door.

"It *is* Number 13, you see," said the latter.

"Yes; there is your door, and there is mine," said Jensen.

"My room has three windows in the daytime," said Anderson, with difficulty suppressing a nervous laugh.

"By George, so has mine!" said the lawyer, turning and looking at Anderson. His back was now to the door. In that moment the door opened, and an arm came out and clawed at his shoulder. It was clad in ragged, yellowish linen, and the bare skin, where it could be seen, had long gray hair upon it.

Anderson was just in time to pull Jensen out of its reach with a cry of disgust and fright, when the door shut again, and a low laugh was heard.

Jensen had seen nothing, but when Anderson hurriedly told him what a risk he had run, he fell into a great state of agitation, and suggested that they should retire from the enterprise, and lock themselves up in one or other of their rooms.

However, while he was developing this plan, the landlord and two able-bodied men arrived on the scene, all looking rather serious and alarmed. Jensen met them with a torrent of description and explanation, which did not at all tend to encourage them for the fray.

The men dropped the crowbars they had brought, and said flatly that they were not going to risk their throats in that devil's den. The landlord was miserably nervous and undecided, conscious that if the danger were not faced his hotel was ruined, and very loath to face it himself. Luckily Anderson hit upon a way of rallying the demoralized force.

"Is this," he said, "the Danish courage I have heard so much of? It isn't a German in there, and if it was, we are five to one."

The two servants and Jensen were stung into action by this, and made a dash at the door.

"Stop!" said Anderson. "Don't lose your heads. You stay out here with the light, landlord, and one of you two men break in the door, and don't go in when it gives way."

The men nodded, and the younger stepped forward, raised his crowbar, and dealt a tremendous blow on the upper panel. The result was not in the least what any of them anticipated. There was no cracking or rending of wood — only a dull sound, as if the solid wall had been struck. The man dropped his tool with a shout, and began rubbing his elbow. His cry drew their eyes upon him for a moment; then Anderson looked at the door again. It was gone; the plaster wall of the passage stared him in the face, with a considerable gash in it where the crowbar had struck it. Number 13 had passed out of existence.

For a brief space they stood perfectly still, gazing at the blank wall. An early cock in the yard beneath was heard to crow; and as Anderson glanced in the direction of the sound, he saw through the window at the end of the long passage that the eastern sky was paling to the dawn.

*****

"Perhaps," said the landlord, with hesitation, "you gentleman would like another room for to-night — a double-bedded one?"

Neither Jensen nor Anderson was averse to the suggestion. They felt inclined to hunt in couples after their late experience. It was found convenient, when each of them went to his room to collect the articles he wanted for the night, that the other should go with him and hold the candle. They noticed that both Number 12 and Number 14 had *three* windows.

*****

Next morning the same party re-assembled in Number 12. The landlord was naturally anxious to avoid engaging outside help, and yet it was imperative that the mystery attaching to that part of the house should be cleared up. Accordingly the two servants had been induced to take upon them the function of carpenters. The furniture was cleared away, and, at the cost of a good many irretrievably damaged planks, that portion of the floor was taken up which lay nearest to Number 14.

You will naturally suppose that a skeleton — say that of Mag. Nicolas Francken — was discovered. That was not so. What they did find lying between the beams which supported the flooring was a small copper box. In it was a neatly-folded vellum document, with about twenty lines of writing. Both Anderson and Jensen (who proved to be something of a palæographer) were much excited by this discovery, which promised to afford the key to these extraordinary phenomena.

*****

I possess a copy of an astrological work which I have never read. It has, by way of frontispiece, a woodcut by Hans Sebald Beham, representing a number of sages seated round a table. This detail may enable connoisseurs to identify the book. I cannot myself recollect its title, and it is not at this moment within reach; but the fly-leaves of it are covered with writing, and, during the ten years in which I have owned the volume, I have not been able to determine which way up this writing ought to be read, much less in what language it is. Not dissimilar was the position of Anderson and Jensen after the protracted examination to which they submitted the document in the copper box.

After two days' contemplation of it, Jensen, who was the bolder spirit of the two, hazarded the conjecture that the language was either Latin or Old Danish.

Anderson ventured upon no surmises, and was very willing to surrender the box and the parchment to the Historical Society of Viborg to be placed in their museum.

I had the whole story from him a few months later, as we sat in a wood near Upsala, after a visit to the library there, where we — or, rather, I — had laughed over the contract by which Daniel Salthenius (in later life Professor of Hebrew at Königsberg) sold himself to Satan. Anderson was not really amused.

"Young idiot!" he said, meaning Salthenius, who was only an undergraduate when he committed that indiscretion, "how did he know what company he was courting?"

And when I suggested the usual considerations he only grunted. That same afternoon he told me what you have read; but he refused to draw any inferences from it, and to assent to any that I drew for him.

III. Joseph a Story — Katherine Rickford

They were sitting round the fire after dinner — not an ordinary fire, one of those fires that has a little room all to itself with seats at each side of it to hold a couple of people or three.

The big dining-room was panelled with oak. At the far end was a handsome dresser that dated back for generations. One's imagination ran riot when one pictured the people who must have laid those pewter plates on the long, narrow, solid table. Massive, mediæval chests stood against the walls. Arms and parts of armour hung against the panelling; but one noticed few of these things, for there was no light in the room save what the fire gave.

It was Christmas Eve. Games had been played. The old had vied with the young at snatching raisins from the burning snapdragon. The children had long since gone to bed; it was time their elders followed them, but they lingered round the fire, taking turns at telling stories. Nothing very weird had been told; no one had felt any wish to peep over his shoulder or try to penetrate the darkness of the far end of the room; the omission caused a sensation of something wanting. From each one there this thought went out, and so a sudden silence fell upon the party. It was a girl who broke it — a mere child; she wore her hair up that night for the first time, and that seemed to give her the right to sit up so late.

"Mr. Grady is going to tell one," she said.

All eyes were turned to a middle-aged man in a deep armchair placed straight in front of the fire. He was short, inclined to be fat, with a bald head and a pointed beard like the beards that sailors wear. It was plain that he was deeply conscious of the sudden turning of so much strained yet forceful thought upon himself. He was restless in his chair as people are in a room that is overheated. He blinked his eyes as he looked round the company. His lips twitched in a nervous manner. One side of him seemed to be endeavouring to restrain another side of him from a feverish desire to speak.

"It was this room that made me think of him," he said thoughtfully.

There was a long silence, but it occurred to no one to prompt him. Everyone seemed to understand that he was going to speak, or rather that something inside him was going to speak, some force that craved expression and was using him as a medium.

The little old man's pink face grew strangely calm, the animation that usually lit it was gone. One would have said that the girl who had started him already regretted the impulse, and now wanted to stop him. She was breathing heavily, and once or twice made as though she would speak to him, but no words came. She must have abandoned the idea, for she fell to studying the company. She examined them carefully, one by one. "This one," she told herself, "is so-and-so, and that one there just another so-and-so." She stared at them, knowing that she could not turn them to herself with her stare. They were just bodies kept working, so to speak, by some subtle sort of sentry left behind by the real selves that streamed out in pent-up thought to the little old man in the chair in front of the fire.

"His name was Joseph: at least they called him Joseph. He dreamed, you understand — dreams. He was an extraordinary lad in many ways. His mother

— I knew her very well — had three children in quick succession, soon after marriage; then ten years went by and Joseph was born. Quiet and reserved he always was, a self-contained child whose only friend was his mother. People said things about him, you know how people talk. Some said he was not Clara's child at all, but that she had adopted him; others, that her husband was not his father, and these put her change of manner down to a perpetual struggle to keep her husband comfortably in the dark. I always imagined that the boy was in some way aware of all this gossip, for I noticed that he took a dislike to the people who spread it most."

The little man rested his elbows on the arms of his chair and let the tips of his fingers meet in front of him. A smile played about his mouth. He seemed to be searching among his reminiscences for the one that would give the clearest portrait of Joseph.

"Well, anyway," he said at last, "the boy was odd, there is no gainsaying the fact. I suppose he was eleven when Clara came down here with her family for Christmas. The Coningtons owned the place then — Mrs. Conington was Clara's sister. It was Christmas Eve, as it is now, many years ago. We had spent a normal Christmas Eve; a little happier, perhaps, than usual by reason of the family reunion and because of the presence of so many children. We had eaten and drank, laughed and played and gone to bed.

"I woke in the middle of the night from sheer restlessness. Clara, knowing my weakness, had given me a fire in my room. I lit a cigarette, played with a book, and then, purely from curiosity, opened the door and looked down the passage. From my door I could see the head of the staircase in the distance; the opposite wing of the house, or the passage rather beyond the stairs, was in darkness. The reason I saw the staircase at all was that the window you pass coming downstairs allowed the moon to throw an uncertain light upon it, a weird light because of the stained glass. I was arrested by the curious effect of this patch of light in so much darkness when suddenly someone came into it, turned, and went downstairs. It was just like a scene in a theatre; something was about to happen that I was going to miss. I ran as I was, barefooted, to the head of the stairs and looked over the banister. I was excited, strung up, too strung up to feel the fright that I knew must be with me. I remember the sensation perfectly. I knew that I was afraid, yet I did not feel fright.

"On the stairs nothing moved. The little hall down here was lost in darkness. Looking over the banister I was facing the stained glass window. You know how the stairs run round three sides of the hall; well, it occurred to me that if I went half-way down and stood under the window I should be able to keep the top of the stairs in sight and see anything that might happen in the hall. I crept down very cautiously and waited under the window. First of all, I saw the suit of empty armour just outside the door here. You know how a thing like that, if you stare at it in a poor light, appears to move; well, it moved sure enough, and the illusion was enhanced by clouds being blown across the moon. By the fire like this one can talk of these things rationally, but in the dead of night it is a different matter, so I went down a few steps to make sure of that armour, when suddenly something passed me on the stairs. I did not hear it, I did not see it, I sensed it in no way, I just knew that something had passed me on its way upstairs. I realized that my retreat was cut off, and with the knowledge fear came upon me.

"I had seen someone come down the stairs; that, at any rate, was definite; now I wanted to see him again. Any ghost is bad enough, but a ghost that one can see is better than one that one can't. I managed to get past the suit of armour, but then I had to feel my way to these double doors here."

He indicated the direction of the doors by a curious wave of his hand. He did not look toward them nor did any of the party. Both men and women were completely absorbed in his story, they seemed to be mesmerized by the earnestness of his manner. Only the girl was restless, she gave an impression of impatience with the slowness with which he came to his point. One would have said that she was apart from her fellows, an alien among strangers.

"So dense was the darkness that I made sure of finding the first door closed, but it was not, it was wide open, and, standing between them, I could feel that the other was open, too. I was standing literally in the wall of the house, and as I peered into the room, trying to make out some familiar object, thoughts ran through my mind of people who had been bricked up in walls and left there to die. For a moment I caught the spirit of the inside of a thick wall. Then suddenly I felt the sensation I have often read about but never experienced before: I knew there was someone in the room. You are surprised, yes, but wait! I knew more: I knew that that someone was conscious of my presence. It occurred to me that whoever it was might want to get out of the door. I made room for him to pass. I waited for him, made sure of him, began to feel giddy, and then a man's voice, deep and clear:

"'There is someone there; who is it?'

"I answered mechanically: 'George Grady.'

"'I'm Joseph.'

"A match was drawn across a match-box, and I saw the boy bending over a candle waiting for the wick to catch. For a moment I thought he must be walking in his sleep, but he turned to me quite naturally and said in his own boyish voice:

"'Lost anything?'

"I was amazed at the lad's complete calm. I wanted to share my fright with someone, instead I had to hide it from this boy. I was conscious of a curious sense of shame. I had watched him grow, taught him, praised him, scolded him, and yet here he was waiting for an explanation of my presence in the dining-room at that odd hour of the night.

"Soon he repeated the question: 'Lost anything?'

"'No,' I said, and then I stammered: 'Have you?'

"'No,' he said with a little laugh. 'It's that room, I can't sleep in it.'

"'Oh,' I said. 'What's the matter with the room?'

"'It's the room I was killed in,' he said quite simply.

"Of course I had heard about his dreams, but I had had no direct experience of them; when, therefore, he said that he had been killed in his room I took it for granted that he had been dreaming again. I was at a loss to know quite how to tackle him; whether to treat the whole thing as absurd and laugh it off as such, or whether to humour him and hear his story. I got him upstairs to my room, sat him in a big armchair, and poked the fire into a blaze.

"'You've been dreaming again,' I said bluntly.

"'Oh, no I haven't. Don't you run away with that idea.'

"His whole manner was so grown up that it was quite unthinkable to treat him as the child he really was. In fact, it was a little uncanny, this man in a child's frame.

"'I was killed there,' he said again.

"'How do you mean killed?' I asked him.

"'Why, killed — murdered. Of course it was years and years ago, I can't say when; still I remember the room. I suppose it was the room that reminded me of the incident.'

"'Incident!' I exclaimed.

"'What else? Being killed is only an incident in the existence of anyone. One makes a fuss about it at the time, of course, but really when you come to think of it...'

"'Tell me about it,' I said, lighting a cigarette. He lit one too, that child, and began.

"'You know my room is the only modern one in this old house. Nobody knows why it is modern. The reason is obvious. Of course it was made modern after I was killed there. The funny thing is that I should have been put there. I suppose it was done for a purpose, because I — I — '

"He looked at me so fixedly I knew he would catch me if I lied.

"'What,' I asked.

"'Dream.'

"'Yes,' I said, 'that is why you were put there.'

"'I thought so, and yet of all the rooms — but then, of course, no one knew. Anyhow I did not recognize the room until after I was in bed. I had been asleep some time and then I woke suddenly. There is an old wheel-back chair there — the only old thing in the room. It is standing facing the fire as it must have stood the night I was killed. The fire was burning brightly, the pattern of the back of the chair was thrown in shadow across the ceiling. Now the night I was murdered the conditions were exactly the same, so directly I saw that pattern on the ceiling I remembered the whole thing. I was not dreaming, don't think it, I was not. What happened that night was this: I was lying in bed counting the parts of the back of that chair in shadow on the ceiling. I probably could not get to sleep: you know the sort of thing, count up to a thousand and remember in the morning where you got to. Well, I was counting those pieces when suddenly they were obliterated, the whole back became a shadow, someone was sitting in the chair. Now, surely you understand that directly I saw the shadow of that chair on the ceiling to-night I realized that I had not a moment to lose. At any moment that same person might come back to that same chair and escape would be impossible. I slipped from my bed as quickly as I could and ran downstairs.'

"'But were you not afraid,' I asked,'downstairs?'

"'That she might follow me? It was a woman, you know. No, I don't think I was. She does not belong downstairs. Anyhow she didn't.'

"'No,' I said. 'No.'

"My voice must have been out of control, for he caught me up at once.

"'You don't mean to say you saw her?' he said

vehemently.

"'Oh, no.'

"'You felt her?'

"'She passed me as I came downstairs,' I said.

"'What can I have done to her that she follows me so?' He buried his face in his hands as though searching for an answer to his thought. Suddenly he looked up and stared at me.

"'Where had I got to? Oh yes, the murder. I can remember it all distinctly.

"'You can imagine how startled I was to see that shadow in the chair — startled, you know, but not really frightened. I leaned up in bed and looked at the chair, and sure enough a woman was sitting in it — a young woman. I watched her with a profound interest until she began to turn in her chair, as I felt, to look at me; when she did that I shrank back in bed. I dared not meet her eyes. She might not have had eyes, she might not have had a face. You know the sort of pictures that one sees when one glances back at all one's soul has ever thought.

"'I got back in the bed as far as I could and peeped over the sheets at the shadow on the ceiling. I was tired; frightened to death; I grew weary of watching; I must have fallen asleep, for suddenly the fire was almost out, the pattern of the chair barely discernible, the shadow had gone. I raised myself with a sense of huge relief. Yes, the chair was empty, but, just think of it: the woman was on the floor, on her hands and knees, crawling toward the bed.

"'I fell back stricken with terror.

"'Very soon I felt a gentle pull at the counterpane.

I thought I was in a nightmare but too lazy or too comfortable to try to wake myself from it. I waited in an agony of suspense, but nothing seemed to be happening, in fact I had just persuaded myself that the movement of the counterpane was fancy when a hand brushed softly over my knee. There was no mistaking it, I could feel the long, thin fingers. Now was the time to do something. I tried to rouse myself, but all my efforts were futile, I was stiff from head to foot.

"'Although the hand was lost to me, outwardly, it now came within my range of knowledge, if you know what I mean. I knew that it was groping its way along the bed, feeling for some other part of me. At any moment I could have said exactly where it had got to. When it was hovering just over my chest another hand knocked lightly against my shoulder. I fancied it lost, and wandering in search of its fellow.

"'I was lying on my back staring at the ceiling when the hands met; the weight of their presence brought a feeling of oppression to my chest. I seemed to be completely cut off from my body; I had no sort of connection with any part of it, nothing about me would respond to my will to make it move.

"'There was no sound at all anywhere.

"'I fell into a state of indifference, a sort of patient indifference that can wait for an appointed time to come. How long I waited I cannot say, but when the time came it found me ready. I was not taken by surprise.

"'There was a great upward rush of pent-up force released; it was like a mighty mass of men who have been lost in prayer rising to their feet. I can't remember clearly, but I think the woman must have got on to my bed. I could not follow her distinctly, my whole attention was concentrated on her hands. All the time I felt those fingers itching for my throat.

"'At last they moved; slowly at first, then quicker; and then a long-drawn swish like the sound of an overbold wave that has broken too far up the beach and is sweeping back to join the sea.'

"The boy was silent for a moment, then he stretched out his hand for the cigarettes.

"'You remember nothing else?' I asked him.

"'No,' he said. 'The next thing I remember clearly is deliberately breaking the nursery window because it was raining and mother would not let me go out.'"

There was a moment's tension, then the strain of listening passed and everyone seemed to be speaking at once. The Rector was taking the story seriously.

"Tell me, Grady," he said. "How long do you suppose elapsed between the boy's murder and his breaking the nursery window?"

But a young married woman in the first flush of her happiness broke in between them. She ridiculed the whole idea. Of course the boy was dreaming. She was drawing the majority to her way of thinking when, from the corner where the girl sat, a hollow-sounding voice:

"And the boy? Where is he?"

The tone of the girl's voice inspired horror, that fear that does not know what it is it fears; one could see it on every face; on every face, that is, but the face of the bald-headed little man; there was no horror on his face, he was smiling serenely as he looked the girl straight in the eyes.

"He's a man now," he said.

"Alive?" she cried.

"Why not?" said the little old man, rubbing his hands together.

She tried to rise, but her frock had got caught between the chairs and pulled her to her seat again. The man next her put out his hand to steady her, but she dashed it away roughly. She looked round the party for an instant for all the world like an animal at bay, then she sprang to her feet and charged blindly. They crowded round her to prevent her falling; at the touch of their hands she stopped. She was out of breath as though she had been running.

"All right," she said, pushing their hands from her. "All right. I'll come quietly. I did it."

They caught her as she fell and laid her on the sofa watching the colour fade from her face.

The hostess, an old woman with white hair and a kind face, approached the little old man; for once in her life she was roused to anger.

"I can't think how you could be so stupid," she said. "See what you have done."

"I did it for a purpose," he said.

"For a purpose?"

"I have always thought that girl was the culprit. I have to thank you for the opportunity you have given me of making sure."

IV. The Horla — Guy de Maupassant

May 8th. What a lovely day! I have spent all the morning lying in the grass in front of my house, under the enormous plantain tree which covers it, and shades and shelters the whole of it. I like this part of the country and I am fond of living here because I am attached to it by deep roots, profound and delicate roots which attach a man to the soil on which his ancestors were born and died, which attach him to what people think and what they eat, to the usages as well as to the food, local expression, the peculiar language of the peasants, to the smell of the soil, of the villages and of the atmosphere itself.

I love my house in which I grew up. From my windows I can see the Seine which flows by the side of my garden, on the other side of the road, almost through my grounds, the great and wide Seine which goes to Rouen and Havre, and which is covered with boats passing to and fro.

On the left, down yonder, lies Rouen, that large town with its blue roofs, under its pointed Gothic towers. They are innumerable, delicate or broad, dominated by the spire of the cathedral, and full of bells which sound through the blue air on fine mornings, sending their sweet and distant iron clang to me; their metallic sound which the breeze wafts in my direction, now stronger and now weaker, according as the wind is stronger or lighter.

What a delicious morning it was!

About eleven o'clock, a long line of boats drawn by a steam tug, as big as a fly, and which scarcely puffed while emitting its thick smoke, passed my gate.

After two English schooners, whose red flag fluttered toward the sky, there came a magnificent Brazilian three-master; it was perfectly white and wonderfully clean and shining. I saluted it, I hardly know why, except that the sight of the vessel gave me great pleasure.

May 12th. I have had a slight feverish attack for the last few days, and I feel ill, or rather I feel low-spirited.

Whence do these mysterious influences come, which change our happiness into discouragement, and our self-confidence into diffidence? One might almost say that the air, the invisible air, is full of unknowable Forces, whose mysterious presence we have to endure. I wake up in the best spirits, with an inclination to sing in my throat. Why? I go down by the side of the water, and suddenly, after walking a short distance, I return home wretched, as if some misfortune were awaiting me there. Why? Is it a cold shiver which, passing over my skin, has upset my nerves and given me low spirits? Is it the form of the clouds, or the colour of the sky, or the colour of the surrounding objects which is so changeable, which have troubled my thoughts as they passed before my eyes? Who can tell? Everything that surrounds us, everything that we see without looking at it, everything that we touch without knowing it, everything that we handle without feeling it, all that we meet without clearly distinguishing it, has a rapid, surprising and inexplicable effect upon us and upon our organs, and through them on our ideas and on our heart itself.

How profound that mystery of the Invisible is! We cannot fathom it with our miserable senses, with our eyes which are unable to perceive what is either too small or too great, too near to, or too far from us;

neither the inhabitants of a star nor of a drop of water ... with our ears that deceive us, for they transmit to us the vibrations of the air in sonorous notes. They are fairies who work the miracle of changing that movement into noise, and by that metamorphosis give birth to music, which makes the mute agitation of nature musical ... with our sense of smell which is smaller than that of a dog ... with our sense of taste which can scarcely distinguish the age of a wine!

Oh! If we only had other organs which would work other miracles in our favour, what a number of fresh things we might discover around us!

May 16th. I am ill, decidedly! I was so well last month! I am feverish, horribly feverish, or rather I am in a state of feverish enervation, which makes my mind suffer as much as my body. I have without ceasing that horrible sensation of some danger threatening me, that apprehension of some coming misfortune or of approaching death, that presentiment which is, no doubt, an attack of some illness which is still unknown, which germinates in the flesh and in the blood.

May 18th. I have just come from consulting my medical man, for I could no longer get any sleep. He found that my pulse was high, my eyes dilated, my nerves highly strung, but no alarming symptoms. I must have a course of shower-baths and of bromide of potassium.

May 25th. No change! My state is really very peculiar. As the evening comes on, an incomprehensible feeling of disquietude seizes me, just as if night concealed some terrible menace toward me. I dine quickly, and then try to read, but I do not understand the words, and can scarcely distinguish the letters. Then I walk up and down my drawing-room, oppressed by a feeling of confused and irresistible fear, the fear of sleep and fear of my bed.

About ten o'clock I go up to my room. As soon as I have got in I double lock, and bolt it: I am frightened — of what? Up till the present time I have been frightened of nothing — I open my cupboards, and look under my bed; I listen — I listen — to what? How strange it is that a simple feeling of discomfort, impeded or heightened circulation, perhaps the irritation of a nervous thread, a slight congestion, a small disturbance in the imperfect and delicate functions of our living machinery, can turn the most lighthearted of men into a melancholy one, and make a coward of the bravest! Then, I go to bed, and I wait for sleep as a man might wait for the executioner. I wait for its coming with dread, and my heart beats and my legs tremble, while my whole body shivers beneath the warmth of the bedclothes, until the moment when I suddenly fall asleep, as one would throw oneself into a pool of stagnant water in order to drown oneself. I do not feel coming over me, as I used to do formerly, this perfidious sleep which is close to me and watching me, which is going to seize me by the head, to close my eyes and annihilate me.

I sleep — a long time — two or three hours perhaps — then a dream — no — a nightmare lays hold on me. I feel that I am in bed and asleep — I feel it and I know it — and I feel also that somebody is coming close to me, is looking at me, touching me, is getting on to my bed, is kneeling on my chest, is taking my neck between his hands and squeezing it — squeezing it with all his might in order to strangle me.

I struggle, bound by that terrible powerlessness which paralyzes us in our dreams; I try to cry out —

but I cannot; I want to move — I cannot; I try, with the most violent efforts and out of breath, to turn over and throw off this being which is crushing and suffocating me — I cannot!

And then, suddenly, I wake up, shaken and bathed in perspiration; I light a candle and find that I am alone, and after that crisis, which occurs every night, I at length fall asleep and slumber tranquilly till morning.

June 2d. My state has grown worse. What is the matter with me? The bromide does me no good, and the shower-baths have no effect whatever. Sometimes, in order to tire myself out, though I am fatigued enough already, I go for a walk in the forest of Roumare. I used to think at first that the fresh light and soft air, impregnated with the odour of herbs and leaves, would instill new blood into my veins and impart fresh energy to my heart. I turned into a broad ride in the wood, and then I turned toward La Bouille, through a narrow path, between two rows of exceedingly tall trees, which placed a thick, green, almost black roof between the sky and me.

A sudden shiver ran through me, not a cold shiver, but a shiver of agony, and so I hastened my steps, uneasy at being alone in the wood, frightened stupidly and without reason, at the profound solitude. Suddenly it seemed to me as if I were being followed, that somebody was walking at my heels, close, quite close to me, near enough to touch me.

I turned round suddenly, but I was alone. I saw nothing behind me except the straight, broad ride, empty and bordered by high trees, horribly empty; on the other side it also extended until it was lost in the distance, and looked just the same, terrible.

I closed my eyes. Why? And then I began to turn round on one heel very quickly, just like a top. I nearly fell down, and opened my eyes; the trees were dancing round me and the earth heaved; I was obliged to sit down. Then, ah! I no longer remembered how I had come! What a strange idea! What a strange, strange idea! I did not the least know. I started off to the right, and got back into the avenue which had led me into the middle of the forest.

June 3d. I have had a terrible night. I shall go away for a few weeks, for no doubt a journey will set me up again.

July 2d. I have come back, quite cured, and have had a most delightful trip into the bargain. I have been to Mont Saint-Michel, which I had not seen before.

What a sight, when one arrives as I did, at Avranches toward the end of the day! The town stands on a hill, and I was taken into the public garden at the extremity of the town. I uttered a cry of astonishment. An extraordinary large bay lay extended before me, as far as my eyes could reach, between two hills which were lost to sight in the mist; and in the middle of this immense yellow bay, under a clear, golden sky, a peculiar hill rose up, sombre and pointed in the midst of the sand. The sun had just disappeared, and under the still flaming sky the outline of that fantastic rock stood out, which bears on its summit a fantastic monument.

At daybreak I went to it. The tide was low as it had been the night before, and I saw that wonderful abbey rise up before me as I approached it. After several hours' walking, I reached the enormous mass of rocks which supports the little town, dominated by the great church. Having climbed the steep and narrow street, I entered the most wonderful Gothic building that has ever been built to God on earth, as large as a town, full of low rooms which seem buried beneath vaulted roofs, and lofty galleries supported by delicate columns.

I entered this gigantic granite jewel which is as light as a bit of lace, covered with towers, with slender belfries to which spiral staircases ascend, and which raise their strange heads that bristle with chimeras, with devils, with fantastic animals, with monstrous flowers, and which are joined together by finely carved arches, to the blue sky by day, and to the black sky by night.

When I had reached the summit, I said to the monk who accompanied me: "Father, how happy you must be here!" And he replied: "It is very windy, Monsieur"; and so we began to talk while watching the rising tide, which ran over the sand and covered it with a steel cuirass.

And then the monk told me stories, all the old stories belonging to the place, legends, nothing but legends.

One of them struck me forcibly. The country people, those belonging to the Mornet, declare that at night one can hear talking going on in the sand, and then that one hears two goats bleat, one with a strong, the other with a weak voice. Incredulous people declare that it is nothing but the cry of the sea birds, which occasionally resembles bleatings, and occasionally human lamentations; but belated fishermen swear that they have met an old shepherd, whose head, which is covered by his cloak, they can never see, wandering on the downs, between two tides, round the little town placed so far out of the world, and who is guiding and walking before them, a he-goat with a man's face, and a she-goat with a woman's face, and both of them with white hair; and talking incessantly, quarrelling in a strange language, and then suddenly ceasing to talk in order to bleat with all their might.

"Do you believe it?" I asked the monk. "I scarcely know," he replied, and I continued: "If there are other beings besides ourselves on this earth, how comes it that we have not known it for so long a time, or why have you not seen them? How is it that I have not seen them?" He replied: "Do we see the hundred thousandth part of what exists? Look here; there is the wind, which is the strongest force in nature, which knocks down men, and blows down buildings, uproots trees, raises the sea into mountains of water; destroys cliffs and casts great ships onto the breakers; the wind which kills, which whistles, which sighs, which roars — have you ever seen it, and can you see it? It exists for all that, however."

I was silent before this simple reasoning. The man was a philosopher, or perhaps a fool; I could not say which exactly, so I held my tongue. What he had said, had often been in my own thoughts.

July 3d. I have slept badly; certainly there is some feverish influence here, for my coachman is suffering in the same way as I am. When I went back home yesterday, I noticed his singular paleness, and I asked him: "What is the matter with you, Jean?" "The matter is that I never get any rest, and my nights devour my days. Since your departure, monsieur, there has been a spell over me."

However, the other servants are all well, but I am very frightened of having another attack, myself.

July 4th. I am decidedly taken again; for my old nightmares have returned. Last night I felt somebody leaning on me who was sucking my life from between my lips with his mouth. Yes, he was sucking it out of my neck, like a leech would have done. Then he got up, satiated, and I woke up, so beaten, crushed and annihilated that I could not move. If this continues for a few days, I shall certainly go away again.

July 5th. Have I lost my reason? What has happened? What I saw last night is so strange that my head wanders when I think of it!

As I do now every evening, I had locked my door, and then, being thirsty, I drank half a glass of water, and I accidentally noticed that the water bottle was full up to the cut-glass stopper.

Then I went to bed and fell into one of my terrible sleeps, from which I was aroused in about two hours by a still more terrible shock.

Picture to yourself a sleeping man who is being murdered and who wakes up with a knife in his chest, and who is rattling in his throat, covered with blood, and who can no longer breathe, and is going to die, and does not understand anything at all about it — there it is.

Having recovered my senses, I was thirsty again, so I lit a candle and went to the table on which my water bottle was. I lifted it up and tilted it over my glass, but nothing came out. It was empty! It was completely empty! At first I could not understand it at all, and then suddenly I was seized by such a terrible feeling that I had to sit down, or rather I fell into a chair! Then I sprang up with a bound to look about me, and then I sat down again, overcome by astonishment and fear, in front of the transparent crystal bottle! I looked at it with fixed eyes, trying to conjecture, and my hands trembled! Somebody had drunk the water, but who? I? I without any doubt. It could surely only be I? In that case I was a somnambulist, I lived, without knowing it, that double mysterious life which makes us doubt whether there are not two beings in us, or whether a strange, unknowable and invisible being does not at such moments, when our soul is in a state of torpor, animate our captive body which obeys this other being, as it does us ourselves, and more than it does ourselves.

Oh! Who will understand my horrible agony? Who will understand the emotion of a man who is sound in mind, wide awake, full of sound sense, and who looks in horror at the remains of a little water that has disappeared while he was asleep, through the glass of a water bottle? And I remained there until it was daylight, without venturing to go to bed again.

July 6th. I am going mad. Again all the contents of my water bottle have been drunk during the night — or rather, I have drunk it!

But is it I? Is it I? Who could it be? Who? Oh! God! Am I going mad? Who will save me?

July 10th. I have just been through some surprising ordeals. Decidedly I am mad! And yet! —

On July 6th, before going to bed, I put some wine, milk, water, bread and strawberries on my table. Somebody drank — I drank — all the water and a little of the milk, but neither the wine, bread nor the strawberries were touched.

On the seventh of July I renewed the same experiment, with the same results, and on July 8th, I left out the water and the milk and nothing was touched.

Lastly, on July 9th I put only water and milk on my table, taking care to wrap up the bottles in white muslin and to tie down the stoppers. Then I rubbed my lips, my beard and my hands with pencil lead, and went to bed.

Irresistible sleep seized me, which was soon followed by a terrible awakening. I had not moved, and my sheets were not marked. I rushed to the table. The muslin round the bottles remained intact; I undid the string, trembling with fear. All the water had been drunk, and so had the milk! Ah! Great God! –

I must start for Paris immediately.

July 12th. Paris. I must have lost my head during the last few days! I must be the plaything of my enervated imagination, unless I am really a somnambulist, or that I have been brought under the power of one of those influences which have been proved to exist, but which have hitherto been inexplicable, which are called suggestions. In any case, my mental state bordered on madness, and twenty-four hours of Paris sufficed to restore me to my equilibrium.

Yesterday after doing some business and paying some visits which instilled fresh and invigorating mental air into me, I wound up my evening at the *Théâtre Français*. A play by Alexandre Dumas the Younger was being acted, and his active and powerful mind completed my cure. Certainly solitude is dangerous for active minds. We require men who can think and can talk, around us. When we are alone for a long time we people space with phantoms.

I returned along the boulevards to my hotel in excellent spirits. Amid the jostling of the crowd I thought, not without irony, of my terrors and surmises of the previous week, because I believed, yes, I believed, that an invisible being lived beneath my roof. How weak our head is, and how quickly it is terrified and goes astray, as soon as we are struck by a small, incomprehensible fact.

Instead of concluding with these simple words: "I do not understand because the cause escapes me," we immediately imagine terrible mysteries and supernatural powers.

July 14th. Fête of the Republic. I walked through the streets, and the crackers and flags amused me like a child. Still it is very foolish to be merry on a fixed date, by a Government decree. The populace is an imbecile flock of sheep, now steadily patient, and now in ferocious revolt. Say to it: "Amuse yourself," and it amuses itself. Say to it: "Go and fight with your neighbour," and it goes and fights. Say to it: "Vote for the Emperor," and it votes for the Emperor, and then say to it: "Vote for the Republic," and it votes for the Republic.

Those who direct it are also stupid; but instead of obeying men they obey principles, which can only be stupid, sterile, and false, for the very reason that they are principles, that is to say, ideas which are considered as certain and unchangeable, in this world where one is certain of nothing, since light is an illusion and noise is an illusion.

July 16th. I saw some things yesterday that troubled me very much.

I was dining at my cousin's Madame Sablé, whose husband is colonel of the 76th Chasseurs at Limoges. There were two young women there, one of whom had married a medical man, Dr. Parent, who devotes himself a great deal to nervous diseases and the extraordinary manifestations to which at this moment experiments in hypnotism and suggestion give rise.

He related to us at some length, the enormous results obtained by English scientists and the doctors of the medical school at Nancy, and the facts which he adduced appeared to me so strange, that I declared that I was altogether incredulous.

"We are," he declared, "on the point of discovering one of the most important secrets of nature, I mean to say, one of its most important secrets on this earth, for there are certainly some which are of a different kind of importance up in the stars, yonder. Ever since man has thought, since he has been able to express and write down his thoughts, he has felt himself close to a mystery which is impenetrable to his coarse and imperfect senses, and he endeavours to supplement the want of power of his organs by the efforts of his intellect. As long as that intellect still remained in its elementary stage, this intercourse with invisible spirits assumed forms which were commonplace though terrifying. Thence sprang the popular belief in the supernatural, the legends of wandering spirits, of fairies, of gnomes, ghosts, I might even say the legend of God, for our conceptions of the workman-creator, from whatever religion they may have come down to us, are certainly the most mediocre, the stupidest and the most unacceptable inventions that ever sprang from the frightened brain of any human creatures. Nothing is truer than what Voltaire says: 'God made man in His own image, but man has certainly paid Him back again.'

"But for rather more than a century, men seem to have had a presentiment of something new. Mesmer and some others have put us on an unexpected track, and especially within the last two or three years, we have arrived at really surprising results."

My cousin, who is also very incredulous, smiled, and Dr. Parent said to her: "Would you like me to try and send you to sleep, Madame?" "Yes, certainly."

She sat down in an easy-chair, and he began to look at her fixedly, so as to fascinate her. I suddenly felt myself somewhat uncomfortable, with a beating heart and a choking feeling in my throat. I saw that Madame Sablé's eyes were growing heavy, her mouth twitched and her bosom heaved, and at the end of ten minutes she was asleep.

"Stand behind her," the doctor said to me, and so I took a seat behind her. He put a visiting card into her hands, and said to her: "This is a looking-glass; what do you see in it?" And she replied: "I see my cousin." "What is he doing?" "He is twisting his moustache." "And now?" "He is taking a photograph out of his pocket." "Whose photograph is it?" "His own."

That was true, and that photograph had been given me that same evening at the hotel.

"What is his attitude in this portrait?" "He is standing up with his hat in his hand."

So she saw on that card, on that piece of white pasteboard, as if she had seen it in a looking glass.

The young women were frightened, and exclaimed: "That is quite enough! Quite, quite enough!"

But the doctor said to her authoritatively: "You will get up at eight o'clock to-morrow morning; then you will go and call on your cousin at his hotel and ask him to lend you five thousand francs which your husband demands of you, and which he will ask for when he sets out on his coming journey."

Then he woke her up.

On returning to my hotel, I thought over this curious *séance* and I was assailed by doubts, not as to my cousin's absolute and undoubted good faith, for I had known her as well as if she had been my own sister ever since she was a child, but as to a possible trick on the doctor's part. Had not he, perhaps, kept a glass hidden in his hand, which he showed to the young woman in her sleep, at the same time as he did the card? Professional conjurers do things which are just as singular.

So I went home and to bed, and this morning, at about half past eight, I was awakened by my footman, who said to me: "Madame Sablé has asked to see you immediately, Monsieur," so I dressed hastily and went to her.

She sat down in some agitation, with her eyes on the floor, and without raising her veil she said to me: "My dear cousin, I am going to ask a great favour of you." "What is it, cousin?" "I do not like to tell you, and yet I must. I am in absolute want of five thousand francs." "What, you?" "Yes, I, or rather my husband, who has asked me to procure them for him."

I was so stupefied that I stammered out my answers. I asked myself whether she had not really been making fun of me with Doctor Parent, if it were not merely a very well-acted farce which had been got up beforehand. On looking at her attentively, however, my doubts disappeared. She was trembling with grief, so painful was this step to her, and I was sure that her throat was full of sobs.

I knew that she was very rich and so I continued: "What! Has not your husband five thousand francs at his disposal! Come, think. Are you sure that he commissioned you to ask me for them?"

She hesitated for a few seconds, as if she were making a great effort to search her memory, and then she replied: "Yes ... yes, I am quite sure of it." "He has written to you?"

She hesitated again and reflected, and I guessed the torture of her thoughts. She did not know. She only knew that she was to borrow five thousand francs of me for her husband. So she told a lie. "Yes, he has written to me." "When, pray? You did not mention it to me yesterday." "I received his letter this morning." "Can you show it me?" "No; no ... no ... it contained private matters ... things too personal to ourselves.... I burnt it." "So your husband runs into debt?"

She hesitated again, and then murmured: "I do not know." Thereupon I said bluntly: "I have not five thousand francs at my disposal at this moment, my dear cousin."

She uttered a kind of cry as if she were in pain and said: "Oh! oh! I beseech you, I beseech you to get them for me..."

She got excited and clasped her hands as if she were praying to me! I heard her voice change its tone; she wept and stammered, harassed and dominated by the irresistible order that she had received.

"Oh! oh! I beg you to ... if you knew what I am suffering.... I want them to-day."

I had pity on her: "You shall have them by and by, I swear to you." "Oh! thank you! thank you! How kind you are!"

I continued: "Do you remember what took place

at your house last night?" "Yes." "Do you remember that Doctor Parent sent you to sleep?" "Yes." "Oh! Very well then; he ordered you to come to me this morning to borrow five thousand francs, and at this moment you are obeying that suggestion."

She considered for a few moments, and then replied: "But as it is my husband who wants them..."

For a whole hour I tried to convince her, but could not succeed, and when she had gone I went to the doctor. He was just going out, and he listened to me with a smile, and said: "Do you believe now?" "Yes, I cannot help it." "Let us go to your cousin's."

She was already dozing on a couch, overcome with fatigue. The doctor felt her pulse, looked at her for some time with one hand raised toward her eyes which she closed by degrees under the irresistible power of this influence, and when she was asleep, he said:

"Your husband does not require the five thousand francs any longer! You must, therefore, forget that you asked your cousin to lend them to you, and, if he speaks to you about it, you will not understand him."

Then he woke her up, and I took out a pocket-book and said: "Here is what you asked me for this morning, my dear cousin." But she was so surprised that I did not venture to persist; nevertheless, I tried to recall the circumstance to her, but she denied it vigorously, thought that I was making fun of her, and in the end very nearly lost her temper.

*****

There! I have just come back, and I have not been able to eat any lunch, for this experiment has altogether upset me.

July 19th. Many people to whom I have told the adventure have laughed at me. I no longer know what to think. The wise man says: Perhaps?

July 21st. I dined at Bougival, and then I spent the evening at a boatmen's ball. Decidedly everything depends on place and surroundings. It would be the height of folly to believe in the supernatural on the *île de la Grenouillière* [1] ... but on the top of Mont Saint-Michel?... and in India? We are terribly under the influence of our surroundings. I shall return home next week.

July 30th. I came back to my own house yesterday. Everything is going on well.

August 2d. Nothing fresh; it is splendid weather, and I spend my days in watching the Seine flow past.

August 4th. Quarrels among my servants. They declare that the glasses are broken in the cupboards at night. The footman accuses the cook, who accuses the needlewoman, who accuses the other two. Who is the culprit? A clever person, to be able to tell.

August 6th. This time I am not mad. I have seen ... I have seen ... I have seen!... I can doubt no longer ... I have seen it!...

I was walking at two o'clock among my rose trees, in the full sunlight ... in the walk bordered by autumn roses which are beginning to fall. As I stopped to look at a *Géant de Bataille*, which had three splendid blooms, I distinctly saw the stalk of one of the roses bend, close to me, as if an invisible hand had bent it, and then break, as if that hand had picked it! Then the flower raised itself, following the curve which a hand would have described in carrying it toward a mouth, and it remained suspended in the transparent air, all alone and motionless, a terrible red spot, three yards from my eyes. In desperation I rushed at it to take it! I found nothing; it had disappeared. Then I was seized with furious rage against myself, for it is not allowable for a reasonable and serious man to have such hallucinations.

But was it a hallucination? I turned round to look for the stalk, and I found it immediately under the bush, freshly broken, between two other roses which remained on the branch, and I returned home then, with a much disturbed mind; for I am certain now, as certain as I am of the alternation of day and night, that there exists close to me an invisible being that lives on milk and on water, which can touch objects, take them and change their places; which is, consequently, endowed with a material nature, although it is impossible to our senses, and which lives as I do, under my roof....

August 7th. I slept tranquilly. He drank the water out of my decanter, but did not disturb my sleep.

I ask myself whether I am mad. As I was walking just now in the sun by the riverside, doubts as to my own sanity arose in me; not vague doubts such as I have had hitherto, but precise and absolute doubts. I have seen mad people, and I have known some who have been quite intelligent, lucid, even clear-sighted in every concern of life, except on one point. They spoke clearly, readily, profoundly, on everything, when suddenly their thoughts struck upon the breakers of their madness and broke to pieces there, and were dispersed and foundered in that furious and terrible sea, full of bounding waves, fogs and squalls, which is called *madness*.

I certainly should think that I was mad, absolutely mad, if I were not conscious, did not perfectly know my state, if I did fathom it by analyzing it with the most complete lucidity. I should, in fact, be a reasonable man who was labouring under a hallucination. Some unknown disturbance must have been excited in my brain, one of those disturbances which physiologists of the present day try to note and to fix precisely, and that disturbance must have caused a profound gulf in my mind and in the order and logic of my ideas. Similar phenomena occur in the dreams which lead us through the most unlikely phantasmagoria, without causing us any surprise, because our verifying apparatus and our sense of control has gone to sleep, while our imaginative faculty wakes and works. Is it not possible that one of the imperceptible keys of the cerebral finger-board has been paralyzed in me? Some men lose the recollection of proper names, or of verbs, or of numbers, or merely of dates, in consequence of an accident. The localization of all the particles of thought has been proved nowadays; what then would there be surprising in the fact that my faculty of controlling the unreality of certain hallucinations should be destroyed for the time being!

I thought of all this as I walked by the side of the water. The sun was shining brightly on the river and made earth delightful, while it filled my looks with love for life, for the swallows, whose agility is always delightful in my eyes, for the plants by the riverside, whose rustling is a pleasure to my ears.

By degrees, however, an inexplicable feeling of discomfort seized me. It seemed to me as if some unknown force were numbing and stopping me, were preventing me from going farther and were calling me back. I felt that painful wish to return which oppresses you when you have left a beloved invalid at home, and when you are seized by a presentiment that he is worse.

I, therefore, returned in spite of myself, feeling certain that I should find some bad news awaiting me, a letter or a telegram. There was nothing, however, and I was more surprised and uneasy than if I had had another fantastic vision.

August 8th. I spent a terrible evening yesterday. He does not show himself any more, but I feel that he is near me, watching me, looking at me, penetrating me, dominating me, and more redoubtable when he hides himself thus than if he were to manifest his constant and invisible presence by supernatural phenomena. However, I slept.

August 9th. Nothing, but I am afraid.

August 10th. Nothing; what will happen tomorrow?

August 11th. Still nothing; I cannot stop at home with this fear hanging over me and these thoughts in my mind; I shall go away.

August 12th. Ten o'clock at night. All day long I have been trying to get away, and have not been able. I wished to accomplish this simple and easy act of liberty — go out — get into my carriage in order to go to Rouen — and I have not been able to do it. What is the reason?

August 13th. When one is attacked by certain maladies, all the springs of our physical being appear to be broken, all our energies destroyed, all our muscles relaxed, our bones to have become as soft as our flesh, and our blood as liquid as water. I am experiencing that in my moral being in a strange and distressing manner. I have no longer any strength, any courage, any self-control, nor even any power to set my own will in motion. I have no power left to *will* anything, but someone does it for me and I obey.

August 14th. I am lost! Somebody possesses my soul and governs it! Somebody orders all my acts, all my movements, all my thoughts. I am no longer anything in myself, nothing except an enslaved and terrified spectator of all the things which I do. I wish to go out; I cannot. He does not wish to, and so I remain, trembling and distracted, in the armchair in which he keeps me sitting. I merely wish to get up and to rouse myself, so as to think that I am still master of myself: I cannot! I am riveted to my chair, and my chair adheres to the ground in such a manner that no force could move us.

Then suddenly, I must, I must go to the bottom of my garden to pick some strawberries and eat them, and I go there. I pick the strawberries and I eat them! Oh! my God! my God! Is there a God? If there be one, deliver me! save me! succour me! Pardon! Pity! Mercy! Save me! Oh! what sufferings! what torture! what horror!

August 15th. Certainly this is the way in which my poor cousin was possessed and swayed, when she came to borrow five thousand francs of me. She was under the power of a strange will which had entered into her, like another soul, like another parasitic and ruling soul. Is the world coming to an end?

But who is he, this invisible being that rules me? This unknowable being, this rover of a supernatural race?

Invisible beings exist, then! How is it then that since the beginning of the world they have never manifested themselves in such a manner precisely as they do to me? I have never read anything which resembles what goes on in my house. Oh! If I could only leave it, if I could only go away and flee, so as never to return, I should be saved; but I cannot.

August 16th. I managed to escape to-day for two hours, like a prisoner who finds the door of his dungeon accidentally open. I suddenly felt that I was free and that he was far away, and so I gave orders to put the horses in as quickly as possible, and I drove to Rouen. Oh! How delightful to be able to say to a man who obeyed you: "Go to Rouen!"

I made him pull up before the library, and I begged them to lend me Dr. Herrmann Herestauss's treatise on the unknown inhabitants of the ancient and modern world.

Then, as I was getting into my carriage, I intended to say: "To the railway station!" but instead of this I shouted — I did not say, but I shouted — in such a loud voice that all the passers-by turned round: "Home!" and I fell back onto the cushion of my carriage, overcome by mental agony. He had found me out and regained possession of me.

August 17th. Oh! What a night! what a night! And yet it seems to me that I ought to rejoice. I read until one o'clock in the morning! Herestauss, Doctor of Philosophy and Theogony, wrote the history and the manifestation of all those invisible beings which hover around man, or of whom he dreams. He describes their origin, their domains, their power; but none of them resembles the one which haunts me. One might say that man, ever since he has thought, has had a foreboding of, and feared a new being, stronger than himself, his successor in this world, and that, feeling him near, and not being able to foretell the nature of that master, he has, in his terror, created the whole race of hidden beings, of vague phantoms born of fear.

Having, therefore, read until one o'clock in the morning, I went and sat down at the open window, in order to cool my forehead and my thoughts, in the calm night air. It was very pleasant and warm! How I should have enjoyed such a night formerly!

There was no moon, but the stars darted out their rays in the dark heavens. Who inhabits those worlds? What forms, what living beings, what animals are there yonder? What do those who are thinkers in those distant worlds know more than we do? What can they do more than we can? What do they see which we do not know? Will not one of them, some day or other, traversing space, appear on our earth to conquer it, just as the Norsemen formerly crossed the sea in order to subjugate nations more feeble than themselves?

We are so weak, so unarmed, so ignorant, so small, we who live on this particle of mud which turns round in a drop of water.

I fell asleep, dreaming thus in the cool night air, and then, having slept for about three quarters of an hour, I opened my eyes without moving, awakened by I know not what confused and strange sensation. At first I saw nothing, and then suddenly it appeared to me as if a page of a book which had remained open on my table, turned over of its own accord. Not a breath of air had come in at my window, and I was surprised and waited. In about four minutes, I saw, I saw, yes I saw with my own eyes another page lift itself up and fall down on the others, as if a finger had turned it over. My armchair was empty, appeared empty, but I knew that he was there, he, and sitting in my place, and that he was reading. With a furious bound, the bound of an enraged wild beast that wishes to disembowel its tamer, I crossed my room to seize him, to strangle him, to kill him!... But before I could reach it, my chair fell over as if somebody had run away from me ... my table rocked, my lamp fell and went out, and my window closed as if some thief had been surprised and had fled out into the night, shutting it behind him.

So he had run away: he had been afraid; he, afraid of me!

So ... so ... to-morrow ... or later ... some day or other ... I should be able to hold him in my clutches and crush him against the ground! Do not dogs occasionally bite and strangle their masters?

August 18th. I have been thinking the whole day long. Oh! yes, I will obey him, follow his impulses, fulfill all his wishes, show myself humble, submissive, a coward. He is the stronger; but an hour will come...

August 19th. I know, ... I know ... I know all! I have just read the following in the *Revue de Monde Scientifique*: "A curious piece of news comes to us from Rio de Janeiro. Madness, an epidemic of madness, which may be compared to that contagious madness which attacked the people of Europe in the Middle Ages, is at this moment raging in the Province of San-Paulo. The frightened inhabitants are leaving their houses, deserting their villages, abandoning their land, saying that they are pursued, possessed, governed like human cattle by invisible, though tangible beings, a species of vampire, which feed on their life while they are asleep, and who, besides, drink water and milk without appearing to touch any other nourishment.

"Professor Dom Pedro Henriques, accompanied by several medical savants, has gone to the Province of San-Paulo, in order to study the origin and the manifestations of this surprising madness on the spot, and to propose such measures to the Emperor as may appear to him to be most fitted to restore the mad population to reason."

Ah! Ah! I remember now that fine Brazilian three-master which passed in front of my windows as it was going up the Seine, on the 8th of last May! I thought it looked so pretty, so white and bright! That Being was on board of her, coming from there, where its race sprang from. And it saw me! It saw my house which was also white, and it sprang from the ship onto the land. Oh! Good heavens!

Now I know, I can divine. The reign of man is over, and he has come. He whom disquieted priests exorcised, whom sorcerers evoked on dark nights, without yet seeing him appear, to whom the presentiments of the transient masters of the world lent all the monstrous or graceful forms of gnomes, spirits, genii, fairies, and familiar spirits. After the coarse conceptions of primitive fear, more clear-sighted men foresaw it more clearly. Mesmer divined him, and ten years ago physicians accurately discovered the nature of his power, even before he exercised it himself. They played with that weapon of their new Lord, the sway of a mysterious will over the human soul, which had become enslaved. They called it magnetism, hypnotism, suggestion ... what do I know? I have seen them amusing themselves like impudent children with this horrible power! Woe to us! Woe to man! He has come, the ... the ... what does he call himself ... the ... I fancy that he is shouting out his name to me and I do not hear him ... the ... yes ... he is shouting it out ... I am listening ... I cannot ... repeat ... it ... Horla ... I have heard ... the Horla ... it is he ... the Horla ... he has come!...

Ah! the vulture has eaten the pigeon, the wolf has eaten the lamb; the lion has devoured the buffalo with sharp horns; man has killed the lion with an arrow, with a sword, with gunpowder; but the Horla will make of man what we have made of the horse and of the ox: his chattel, his slave and his food, by the mere power of his will. Woe to us!

But, nevertheless, the animal sometimes revolts and kills the man who has subjugated it.... I should also like ... I shall be able to ... but I must know him, touch him, see him! Learned men say that beasts' eyes, as they differ from ours, do not distinguish like ours do.... And my eye cannot distinguish this newcomer who is oppressing me.

Why? Oh! Now I remember the words of the monk at Mont Saint-Michel: "Can we see the hundred-thousandth part of what exists? Look here; there is the wind which is the strongest force in nature, which knocks down men, and blows down buildings, uproots trees, raises the sea into mountains of water, destroys cliffs and casts great ships onto the breakers; the wind which kills, which whistles, which sighs, which roars — have you ever seen it, and can you see it? It exists for all that, however!"

And I went on thinking: my eyes are so weak, so imperfect, that they do not even distinguish hard bodies, if they are as transparent as glass!... If a glass without tinfoil behind it were to bar my way, I should run into it, just as a bird which has flown into a room breaks its head against the window panes. A thousand things, moreover, deceive him and lead him astray. How should it then be surprising that he cannot perceive a fresh body which is traversed by the light?

A new being! Why not? It was assuredly bound to come! Why should we be the last? We do not distinguish it, like all the others created before us. The reason is, that its nature is more perfect, its body finer and more finished than ours, that ours is so weak, so awkwardly conceived, encumbered with organs that are always tired, always on the strain like locks that are too complicated, which lives like a plant and like a beast, nourishing itself with difficulty on air, herbs and flesh, an animal machine which is a prey to maladies, to malformations, to decay; broken-winded, badly regulated, simple and eccentric, ingeniously badly made, a coarse and a delicate work, the outline of a being which might become intelligent and grand.

We are only a few, so few in this world, from the oyster up to man. Why should there not be one more, when once that period is accomplished which separates the successive apparitions from all the different species?

Why not one more? Why not, also, other trees with immense, splendid flowers, perfuming whole regions? Why not other elements besides fire, air, earth and water? There are four, only four, those nursing fathers of various beings! What a pity! Why are they not forty, four hundred, four thousand! How poor everything is, how mean and wretched! grudgingly given, dryly invented, clumsily made! Ah! the elephant and the hippopotamus, what grace! And the camel, what elegance!

But, the butterfly you will say, a flying flower! I dream of one that should be as large as a hundred worlds, with wings whose shape, beauty, colours, and motion I cannot even express. But I see it ... it flutters from star to star, refreshing them and perfuming them with the light and harmonious breath of its flight!... And the people up there look at it as it passes in an ecstasy of delight!...

What is the matter with me? It is he, the Horla who haunts me, and who makes me think of these foolish things! He is within me, he is becoming my soul; I shall kill him!

August 19th. I shall kill him. I have seen him! Yesterday I sat down at my table and pretended to write very assiduously. I knew quite well that he would come prowling round me, quite close to me, so close that I might perhaps be able to touch him, to seize him. And then!... then I should have the strength of desperation; I should have my hands, my knees, my chest, my forehead, my teeth to strangle him, to crush him, to bite him, to tear him to pieces. And I watched for him with all my overexcited organs.

I had lighted my two lamps and the eight wax candles on my mantelpiece, as if by this light I could have discovered him.

My bed, my old oak bed with its columns, was opposite to me; on my right was the fireplace; on my left the door which was carefully closed, after I had left it open for some time, in order to attract him; behind me was a very high wardrobe with a looking-glass in it, which served me to make my toilet every day, and in which I was in the habit of looking at myself from head to foot every time I passed it.

So I pretended to be writing in order to deceive

him, for he also was watching me, and suddenly I felt, I was certain that he was reading over my shoulder, that he was there, almost touching my ear.

I got up so quickly, with my hands extended, that I almost fell. Eh! well?... It was as bright as at midday, but I did not see myself in the glass!... It was empty, clear, profound, full of light! But my figure was not reflected in it ... and I, I was opposite to it! I saw the large, clear glass from top to bottom, and I looked at it with unsteady eyes; and I did not dare to advance; I did not venture to make a movement, nevertheless, feeling perfectly that he was there, but that he would escape me again, he whose imperceptible body had absorbed my reflection.

How frightened I was! And then suddenly I began to see myself through a mist in the depths of the looking-glass, in a mist as it were through a sheet of water; and it seemed to me as if this water were flowing slowly from left to right, and making my figure clearer every moment. It was like the end of an eclipse. Whatever it was that hid me, did not appear to possess any clearly defined outlines, but a sort of opaque transparency, which gradually grew clearer.

At last I was able to distinguish myself completely, as I do every day when I look at myself.

I had seen it! And the horror of it remained with me and makes me shudder even now.

August 20th. How could I kill it, as I could not get hold of it? Poison? But it would see me mix it with the water; and then, would our poisons have any effect on its impalpable body? No ... no ... no doubt about the matter.... Then?... then?...

August 21st. I sent for a blacksmith from Rouen,

and ordered iron shutters of him for my room, such as some private hotels in Paris have on the ground floor, for fear of thieves, and he is going to make me a similar door as well. I have made myself out as a coward, but I do not care about that!...

September 10th. Rouen, Hotel Continental. It is done; ... it is done ... but is he dead? My mind is thoroughly upset by what I have seen.

Well, then, yesterday the locksmith having put on the iron shutters and door, I left everything open until midnight, although it was getting cold.

Suddenly I felt that he was there and joy, mad joy, took possession of me. I got up softly, and I walked to the right and left for some time, so that he might not guess anything; then I took off my boots and put on my slippers carelessly; then I fastened the iron shutters and going back to the door quickly I double-locked it with a padlock, putting the key into my pocket.

Suddenly I noticed that he was moving restlessly round me, that in his turn he was frightened and was ordering me to let him out. I nearly yielded, though I did not yet, but putting my back to the door I half opened it, just enough to allow me to go out backward, and as I am very tall, my head touched the lintel. I was sure that he had not been able to escape, and I shut him up quite alone, quite alone. What happiness! I had him fast. Then I ran downstairs; in the drawing-room, which was under my bedroom, I took the two lamps and I poured all the oil onto the carpet, the furniture, everywhere; then I set fire to it and made my escape, after having carefully double-locked the door.

I went and hid myself at the bottom of the garden in a clump of laurel bushes. How long it was! how long it was! Everything was dark, silent, motionless, not a breath of air and not a star, but heavy banks of clouds which one could not see, but which weighed, oh! so heavily on my soul.

I looked at my house and waited. How long it was! I already began to think that the fire had gone out of its own accord, or that he had extinguished it, when one of the lower windows gave way under the violence of the flames, and a long, soft, caressing sheet of red flame mounted up the white wall and kissed it as high as the roof. The light fell onto the trees, the branches, and the leaves, and a shiver of fear pervaded them also! The birds awoke; a dog began to howl, and it seemed to me as if the day were breaking! Almost immediately two other windows flew into fragments, and I saw that the whole of the lower part of my house was nothing but a terrible furnace. But a cry, a horrible, shrill, heartrending cry, a woman's cry, sounded through the night, and two garret windows were opened! I had forgotten the servants! I saw the terrorstruck faces, and their frantically waving arms!...

Then, overwhelmed with horror, I set off to run to the village, shouting: "Help! help! fire! fire!" I met some people who were already coming onto the scene, and I went back with them to see!

By this time the house was nothing but a horrible and magnificent funeral pile, a monstrous funeral pile which lit up the whole country, a funeral pile where men were burning, and where he was burning also, He, He, my prisoner, that new Being, the new master, the Horla!

Suddenly the whole roof fell in between the

walls, and a volcano of flames darted up to the sky. Through all the windows which opened onto that furnace I saw the flames darting, and I thought that he was there, in that kiln, dead.

Dead? perhaps?... His body? Was not his body, which was transparent, indestructible by such means as would kill ours?

If he was not dead?... Perhaps time alone has power over that Invisible and Redoubtable Being. Why this transparent, unrecognizable body, this body belonging to a spirit, if it also had to fear ills, infirmities and premature destruction?

Premature destruction? All human terror springs from that! After man the Horla. After him who can die every day, at any hour, at any moment, by any accident, he came who was only to die at his own proper hour and minute, because he had touched the limits of his existence!

No ... no ... without any doubt ... he is not dead. Then ... then ... I suppose I must kill myself!

*****

[1] Frog Island.

V. The Beas With Five Fingers — William F. Harvey

When I was a little boy I once went with my father to call on Adrian Borlsover. I played on the floor with a black spaniel while my father appealed for a subscription. Just before we left my father said, "Mr. Borlsover, may my son here shake hands with you? It will be a thing to look back upon with pride when he grows to be a man."

I came up to the bed on which the old man was lying and put my hand in his, awed by the still beauty of his face. He spoke to me kindly, and hoped that I should always try to please my father. Then he placed his right hand on my head and asked for a blessing to rest upon me. "Amen!" said my father, and I followed him out of the room, feeling as if I wanted to cry. But my father was in excellent spirits.

"That old gentleman, Jim," said he, "is the most wonderful man in the whole town. For ten years he has been quite blind."

"But I saw his eyes," I said. "They were ever so black and shiny; they weren't shut up like Nora's puppies. Can't he see at all?"

And so I learnt for the first time that a man might have eyes that looked dark and beautiful and shining without being able to see.

"Just like Mrs. Tomlinson has big ears," I said, "and can't hear at all except when Mr. Tomlinson shouts."

"Jim," said my father, "it's not right to talk about a lady's ears. Remember what Mr. Borlsover said about pleasing me and being a good boy."

That was the only time I saw Adrian Borlsover. I

soon forgot about him and the hand which he laid in blessing on my head. But for a week I prayed that those dark tender eyes might see.

"His spaniel may have puppies," I said in my prayers, "and he will never be able to know how funny they look with their eyes all closed up. Please let old Mr. Borlsover see."

*****

Adrian Borlsover, as my father had said, was a wonderful man. He came of an eccentric family. Borlsovers' sons, for some reason, always seemed to marry very ordinary women, which perhaps accounted for the fact that no Borlsover had been a genius, and only one Borlsover had been mad. But they were great champions of little causes, generous patrons of odd sciences, founders of querulous sects, trustworthy guides to the bypath meadows of erudition.

Adrian was an authority on the fertilization of orchids. He had held at one time the family living at Borlsover Conyers, until a congenital weakness of the lungs obliged him to seek a less rigorous climate in the sunny south coast watering-place where I had seen him. Occasionally he would relieve one or other of the local clergy. My father described him as a fine preacher, who gave long and inspiring sermons from what many men would have considered unprofitable texts. "An excellent proof," he would add, "of the truth of the doctrine of direct verbal inspiration."

Adrian Borlsover was exceedingly clever with his hands. His penmanship was exquisite. He illustrated all his scientific papers, made his own woodcuts, and carved the reredos that is at present the chief feature of interest in the church at Borlsover Conyers. He had an exceedingly clever knack in cutting silhouettes for young ladies and paper pigs and cows for little children, and made more than one complicated wind instrument of his own devising.

When he was fifty years old Adrian Borlsover lost his sight. In a wonderfully short time he had adapted himself to the new conditions of life. He quickly learned to read Braille. So marvellous indeed was his sense of touch that he was still able to maintain his interest in botany. The mere passing of his long supple fingers over a flower was sufficient means for its identification, though occasionally he would use his lips. I have found several letters of his among my father's correspondence. In no case was there anything to show that he was afflicted with blindness, and this in spite of the fact that he exercised undue economy in the spacing of lines. Toward the close of his life the old man was credited with powers of touch that seemed almost uncanny: it has been said that he could tell at once the colour of a ribbon placed between his fingers. My father would neither confirm nor deny the story.

I

Adrian Borlsover was a bachelor. His elder brother George had married late in life, leaving one son, Eustace, who lived in the gloomy Georgian mansion at Borlsover Conyers, where he could work undisturbed in collecting material for his great book on heredity.

Like his uncle, he was a remarkable man. The Borlsovers had always been born naturalists, but Eustace possessed in a special degree the power of systematizing his knowledge. He had received his university education in Germany, and then, after postgraduate work in Vienna and Naples, had travelled for four years in South America and the East, getting together a huge store of material for a new study into the processes of variation.

He lived alone at Borlsover Conyers with Saunders his secretary, a man who bore a somewhat dubious reputation in the district, but whose powers as a mathematician, combined with his business abilities, were invaluable to Eustace.

Uncle and nephew saw little of each other. The visits of Eustace were confined to a week in the summer or autumn: long weeks, that dragged almost as slowly as the bath-chair in which the old man was drawn along the sunny sea front. In their way the two men were fond of each other, though their intimacy would doubtless have been greater had they shared the same religious views. Adrian held to the old-fashioned evangelical dogmas of his early manhood; his nephew for many years had been thinking of embracing Buddhism. Both men possessed, too, the reticence the Borlsovers had always shown, and which their enemies sometimes called hypocrisy. With Adrian it was a reticence as to the things he had left undone; but with Eustace it seemed that the curtain which he was so careful to leave undrawn hid something more than a half-empty chamber.

*****

Two years before his death Adrian Borlsover developed, unknown to himself, the not uncommon power of automatic writing. Eustace made the discovery by accident. Adrian was sitting reading in bed, the forefinger of his left hand tracing the Braille characters, when his nephew noticed that a pencil the old man held in his right hand was moving slowly along the opposite page. He left his seat in the window and sat down beside the bed. The right hand continued to move, and now he could see plainly that they were letters and words which it was forming.

"Adrian Borlsover," wrote the hand, "Eustace Borlsover, George Borlsover, Francis Borlsover, Sigismund Borlsover, Adrian Borlsover, Eustace Borlsover, Saville Borlsover. B, for Borlsover. Honesty is the Best Policy. Beautiful Belinda Borlsover."

"What curious nonsense!" said Eustace to himself.

"King George the Third ascended the throne in 1760," wrote the hand. "Crowd, a noun of multitude; a collection of individuals — Adrian Borlsover, Eustace Borlsover."

"It seems to me," said his uncle, closing the book, "that you had much better make the most of the afternoon sunshine and take your walk now."

"I think perhaps I will," Eustace answered as he picked up the volume. "I won't go far, and when I come back I can read to you those articles in *Nature* about which we were speaking."

He went along the promenade, but stopped at the first shelter, and seating himself in the corner best protected from the wind, he examined the book at leisure. Nearly every page was scored with a meaningless jungle of pencil marks: rows of capital letters, short words, long words, complete sentences, copybook tags. The whole thing, in fact, had the appearance of a copy-book, and on a more careful scrutiny Eustace thought that there was ample evidence to show that the handwriting at the beginning of the book, good though it was, was not nearly so good as the handwriting at the end.

He left his uncle at the end of October, with a promise to return early in December. It seemed to him quite clear that the old man's power of automatic writing was developing rapidly, and for the first time he looked forward to a visit that combined duty with interest.

But on his return he was at first disappointed. His uncle, he thought, looked older. He was listless too, preferring others to read to him and dictating nearly all his letters. Not until the day before he left had Eustace an opportunity of observing Adrian Borlsover's new-found faculty.

The old man, propped up in bed with pillows, had sunk into a light sleep. His two hands lay on the coverlet, his left hand tightly clasping his right. Eustace took an empty manuscript book and placed a pencil within reach of the fingers of the right hand. They snatched at it eagerly; then dropped the pencil to unloose the left hand from its restraining grasp.

"Perhaps to prevent interference I had better hold that hand," said Eustace to himself, as he watched the pencil. Almost immediately it began to write.

"Blundering Borlsovers, unnecessarily unnatural, extraordinarily eccentric, culpably curious."

"Who are you?" asked Eustace, in a low voice.

"Never you mind," wrote the hand of Adrian.

"Is it my uncle who is writing?"

"Oh, my prophetic soul, mine uncle."

"Is it anyone I know?"

"Silly Eustace, you'll see me very soon."

"When shall I see you?"

"When poor old Adrian's dead."

"Where shall I see you?"

"Where shall you not?"

Instead of speaking his next question, Borlsover wrote it. "What is the time?"

The fingers dropped the pencil and moved three or four times across the paper. Then, picking up the pencil, they wrote:

"Ten minutes before four. Put your book away, Eustace. Adrian mustn't find us working at this sort of thing. He doesn't know what to make of it, and I won't have poor old Adrian disturbed. *Au revoir.*"

Adrian Borlsover awoke with a start.

"I've been dreaming again," he said; "such queer dreams of leaguered cities and forgotten towns. You were mixed up in this one, Eustace, though I can't remember how. Eustace, I want to warn you. Don't walk in doubtful paths. Choose your friends well. Your poor grandfather — "

A fit of coughing put an end to what he was saying, but Eustace saw that the hand was still writing. He managed unnoticed to draw the book away. "I'll light the gas," he said, "and ring for tea." On the other side of the bed curtain he saw the last sentences that had been written.

"It's too late, Adrian," he read. "We're friends already; aren't we, Eustace Borlsover?"

On the following day Eustace Borlsover left. He thought his uncle looked ill when he said goodbye, and the old man spoke despondently of the failure his life had been.

"Nonsense, uncle!" said his nephew. "You have got over your difficulties in a way not one in a hundred thousand would have done. Everyone marvels at your splendid perseverance in teaching your hand to take the place of your lost sight. To me it's been a revelation of the possibilities of education."

"Education," said his uncle dreamily, as if the word had started a new train of thought, "education is good so long as you know to whom and for what purpose you give it. But with the lower orders of men, the base and more sordid spirits, I have grave doubts as to its results. Well, goodbye, Eustace, I may not see you again. You are a true Borlsover, with all the Borlsover faults. Marry, Eustace. Marry some good, sensible girl. And if by any chance I don't see you again, my will is at my solicitor's. I've not left you any legacy, because I know you're well provided for, but I thought you might like to have my books. Oh, and there's just one other thing. You know, before the end people often lose control over themselves and make absurd requests. Don't pay any attention to them, Eustace. Good-bye!" and he held out his hand. Eustace took it. It remained in his a fraction of a second longer than he had expected, and gripped him with a virility that was surprising. There was, too, in its touch a subtle sense of intimacy.

"Why, uncle!" he said, "I shall see you alive and well for many long years to come."

Two months later Adrian Borlsover died.

II

Eustace Borlsover was in Naples at the time. He read the obituary notice in the *Morning Post* on the day announced for the funeral.

"Poor old fellow!" he said. "I wonder where I shall find room for all his books."

The question occurred to him again with greater force when three days later he found himself standing in the library at Borlsover Conyers, a huge room built for use, and not for beauty, in the year of Waterloo by a Borlsover who was an ardent admirer of the great Napoleon. It was arranged on the plan of many college libraries, with tall, projecting bookcases forming deep recesses of dusty silence, fit graves for the old hates of forgotten controversy, the dead passions of forgotten lives. At the end of the room, behind the bust of some unknown eighteenth-century divine, an ugly iron corkscrew stair led to a shelf-lined gallery. Nearly every shelf was full.

"I must talk to Saunders about it," said Eustace. "I suppose that it will be necessary to have the billiard-room fitted up with bookcases."

The two men met for the first time after many weeks in the dining-room that evening.

"Hullo!" said Eustace, standing before the fire with his hands in his pockets. "How goes the world, Saunders? Why these dress togs?" He himself was wearing an old shooting-jacket. He did not believe in mourning, as he had told his uncle on his last visit; and though he usually went in for quiet-coloured ties, he wore this evening one of an ugly red, in order to shock Morton the butler, and to make them thrash out the whole question of mourning for themselves in the servants' hall. Eustace was a true Borlsover. "The world," said Saunders, "goes the same as usual, confoundedly slow. The dress togs are accounted for by an invitation from Captain Lockwood to bridge."

"How are you getting there?"

"I've told your coachman to drive me in your carriage. Any objection?"

"Oh, dear me, no! We've had all things in common for far too many years for me to raise objections at this hour of the day."

"You'll find your correspondence in the library," went on Saunders. "Most of it I've seen to. There are a few private letters I haven't opened. There's also a box with a rat, or something, inside it that came by the evening post. Very likely it's the six-toed beast Terry was sending us to cross with the four-toed albino. I didn't look, because I didn't want to mess up my things, but I should gather from the way it's jumping about that it's pretty hungry."

"Oh, I'll see to it," said Eustace, "while you and the Captain earn an honest penny."

Dinner over and Saunders gone, Eustace went into the library. Though the fire had been lit the room was by no means cheerful.

"We'll have all the lights on at any rate," he said, as he turned the switches. "And, Morton," he added, when the butler brought the coffee, "get me a screwdriver or something to undo this box. Whatever the animal is, he's kicking up the deuce of a row. What is it? Why are you dawdling?"

"If you please, sir, when the postman brought it he told me that they'd bored the holes in the lid at the post-office. There were no breathin' holes in the lid, sir, and they didn't want the animal to die. That is all, sir."

"It's culpably careless of the man, whoever he was," said Eustace, as he removed the screws, "packing an animal like this in a wooden box with no means of getting air. Confound it all! I meant to ask Morton to bring me a cage to put it in. Now I suppose I shall have to get one myself."

He placed a heavy book on the lid from which the screws had been removed, and went into the billiard-room. As he came back into the library with an empty cage in his hand he heard the sound of something falling, and then of something scuttling along the floor.

"Bother it! The beast's got out. How in the world am I to find it again in this library!"

To search for it did indeed seem hopeless. He tried to follow the sound of the scuttling in one of the recesses where the animal seemed to be running behind the books in the shelves, but it was impossible to locate it. Eustace resolved to go on quietly reading. Very likely the animal might gain confidence and show itself. Saunders seemed to have dealt in his usual methodical manner with most of the correspondence. There were still the private letters.

What was that? Two sharp clicks and the lights in the hideous candelabra that hung from the ceiling suddenly went out.

"I wonder if something has gone wrong with the fuse," said Eustace, as he went to the switches by the door. Then he stopped. There was a noise at the other end of the room, as if something was crawling up the iron corkscrew stair. "If it's gone into the gallery," he said, "well and good." He hastily turned on the lights, crossed the room, and climbed up the stair. But he could see nothing. His grandfather had placed a little gate at the top of the stair, so that children could run and romp in the gallery without fear of accident. This Eustace closed, and having considerably narrowed the circle of his search, returned to his desk by the fire.

How gloomy the library was! There was no sense of intimacy about the room. The few busts that an eighteenth-century Borlsover had brought back from the grand tour, might have been in keeping in the old library. Here they seemed out of place. They made the room feel cold, in spite of the heavy red damask curtains and great gilt cornices.

With a crash two heavy books fell from the gallery to the floor; then, as Borlsover looked, another and yet another.

"Very well; you'll starve for this, my beauty!" he said. "We'll do some little experiments on the metabolism of rats deprived of water. Go on! Chuck them down! I think I've got the upper hand." He turned once again to his correspondence. The letter was from the family solicitor. It spoke of his uncle's death and of the valuable collection of books that had been left to him in the will.

"There was one request," he read, "which certainly came as a surprise to me. As you know, Mr. Adrian Borlsover had left instructions that his body was to be buried in as simple a manner as possible at Eastbourne. He expressed a desire that there should be neither wreaths nor flowers of any kind, and hoped that his friends and relatives would not consider it necessary to wear mourning. The day before his death we received a letter cancelling these instructions. He wished his body to be embalmed (he gave us the address of the man we were to employ — Pennifer, Ludgate Hill), with orders that his right hand was to be sent to you, stating that it was at your special request. The other arrangements as to the funeral remained unaltered."

"Good Lord!" said Eustace; "what in the world was the old boy driving at? And what in the name of all that's holy is that?"

Someone was in the gallery. Someone had pulled the cord attached to one of the blinds, and it had rolled up with a snap. Someone must be in the gallery, for a second blind did the same. Someone must be walking round the gallery, for one after the other the blinds sprang up, letting in the moonlight.

"I haven't got to the bottom of this yet," said Eustace, "but I will before the night is very much older," and he hurried up the corkscrew stair. He had just got to the top when the lights went out a second time, and he heard again the scuttling along the floor. Quickly he stole on tiptoe in the dim moonshine in the direction of the noise, feeling as he went for one of the switches. His fingers touched the metal knob at last. He turned on the electric light.

About ten yards in front of him, crawling along the floor, was a man's hand. Eustace stared at it in utter astonishment. It was moving quickly, in the manner of a geometer caterpillar, the five fingers humped up one moment, flattened out the next; the thumb appeared to give a crab-like motion to the whole. While he was looking, too surprised to stir, the hand disappeared round the corner. Eustace ran forward. He no longer saw it, but he could hear it as it squeezed its way behind the books on one of the shelves. A heavy volume had been displaced. There was a gap in the row of books where it had got in. In his fear lest it should escape him again, he seized the first book that came to his hand and plugged it into the hole. Then, emptying two shelves of their contents, he took the wooden boards and propped them up in front to make his barrier doubly sure.

"I wish Saunders was back," he said; "one can't tackle this sort of thing alone." It was after eleven, and there seemed little likelihood of Saunders returning before twelve. He did not dare to leave the shelf unwatched, even to run downstairs to ring the bell. Morton the butler often used to come round about eleven to see that the windows were fastened, but he might not come. Eustace was thoroughly unstrung. At last he heard steps down below.

"Morton!" he shouted; "Morton!"

"Sir?"

"Has Mr. Saunders got back yet?"

"Not yet, sir."

"Well, bring me some brandy, and hurry up about it. I'm up here in the gallery, you duffer."

"Thanks," said Eustace, as he emptied the glass. "Don't go to bed yet, Morton. There are a lot of books that have fallen down by accident; bring them up and put them back in their shelves."

Morton had never seen Borlsover in so talkative a mood as on that night. "Here," said Eustace, when the books had been put back and dusted, "you might hold up these boards for me, Morton. That beast in the box got out, and I've been chasing it all over the place."

"I think I can hear it chawing at the books, sir. They're not valuable, I hope? I think that's the carriage, sir; I'll go and call Mr. Saunders."

It seemed to Eustace that he was away for five minutes, but it could hardly have been more than one when he returned with Saunders. "All right, Morton, you can go now. I'm up here, Saunders."

"What's all the row?" asked Saunders, as he lounged forward with his hands in his pockets. The luck had been with him all the evening. He was completely satisfied, both with himself and with Captain Lockwood's taste in wines. "What's the matter? You look to me to be in an absolute blue funk."

"That old devil of an uncle of mine," began Eustace — "oh, I can't explain it all. It's his hand that's been playing old Harry all the evening. But I've got it cornered behind these books. You've got to help me catch it."

"What's up with you, Eustace? What's the game?"

"It's no game, you silly idiot! If you don't believe me take out one of those books and put your hand in and feel."

"All right," said Saunders; "but wait till I've rolled up my sleeve. The accumulated dust of centuries, eh?" He took off his coat, knelt down, and thrust his arm along the shelf.

"There's something there right enough," he said. "It's got a funny stumpy end to it, whatever it is, and nips like a crab. Ah, no, you don't!" He pulled his hand out in a flash. "Shove in a book quickly. Now it can't get out."

"What was it?" asked Eustace.

"It was something that wanted very much to get hold of me. I felt what seemed like a thumb and forefinger. Give me some brandy."

"How are we to get it out of there?"

"What about a landing net?"

"No good. It would be too smart for us. I tell you,

Saunders, it can cover the ground far faster than I can walk. But I think I see how we can manage it. The two books at the end of the shelf are big ones that go right back against the wall. The others are very thin. I'll take out one at a time, and you slide the rest along until we have it squashed between the end two."

It certainly seemed to be the best plan. One by one, as they took out the books, the space behind grew smaller and smaller. There was something in it that was certainly very much alive. Once they caught sight of fingers pressing outward for a way of escape. At last they had it pressed between the two big books.

"There's muscle there, if there isn't flesh and blood," said Saunders, as he held them together. "It seems to be a hand right enough, too. I suppose this is a sort of infectious hallucination. I've read about such cases before."

"Infectious fiddlesticks!" said Eustace, his face white with anger; "bring the thing downstairs. We'll get it back into the box."

It was not altogether easy, but they were successful at last. "Drive in the screws," said Eustace, "we won't run any risks. Put the box in this old desk of mine. There's nothing in it that I want. Here's the key. Thank goodness, there's nothing wrong with the lock."

"Quite a lively evening," said Saunders. "Now let's hear more about your uncle."

They sat up together until early morning. Saunders had no desire for sleep. Eustace was trying to explain and to forget: to conceal from himself a fear that he had never felt before — the fear of walking alone down the long corridor to his bedroom.

III

"Whatever it was," said Eustace to Saunders on the following morning, "I propose that we drop the subject. There's nothing to keep us here for the next ten days. We'll motor up to the Lakes and get some climbing."

"And see nobody all day, and sit bored to death with each other every night. Not for me, thanks. Why not run up to town? Run's the exact word in this case, isn't it? We're both in such a blessed funk. Pull yourself together, Eustace, and let's have another look at the hand."

"As you like," said Eustace; "there's the key." They went into the library and opened the desk. The box was as they had left it on the previous night.

"What are you waiting for?" asked Eustace.

"I am waiting for you to volunteer to open the lid. However, since you seem to funk it, allow me. There doesn't seem to be the likelihood of any rumpus this morning, at all events." He opened the lid and picked out the hand.

"Cold?" asked Eustace.

"Tepid. A bit below blood-heat by the feel. Soft and supple too. If it's the embalming, it's a sort of embalming I've never seen before. Is it your uncle's hand?"

"Oh, yes, it's his all right," said Eustace. "I should know those long thin fingers anywhere. Put it back in the box, Saunders. Never mind about the screws. I'll lock the desk, so that there'll be no chance of its getting out. We'll compromise by motoring up to town for a week. If we get off soon after lunch we ought to be at Grantham or Stamford by night."

"Right," said Saunders; "and to-morrow – Oh, well, by to-morrow we shall have forgotten all about this beastly thing."

If when the morrow came they had not forgotten, it was certainly true that at the end of the week they were able to tell a very vivid ghost story at the little supper Eustace gave on Hallow E'en.

"You don't want us to believe that it's true, Mr. Borlsover? How perfectly awful!"

"I'll take my oath on it, and so would Saunders here; wouldn't you, old chap?"

"Any number of oaths," said Saunders. "It was a long thin hand, you know, and it gripped me just like that."

"Don't, Mr. Saunders! Don't! How perfectly horrid! Now tell us another one, do. Only a really creepy one, please!"

*****

"Here's a pretty mess!" said Eustace on the following day as he threw a letter across the table to Saunders. "It's your affair, though. Mrs. Merrit, if I understand it, gives a month's notice."

"Oh, that's quite absurd on Mrs. Merrit's part," Saunders replied. "She doesn't know what she's talking about. Let's see what she says."

"Dear Sir," he read, "this is to let you know that I must give you a month's notice as from Tuesday the 13th. For a long time I've felt the place too big for me, but when Jane Parfit and Emma Laidlaw go off with scarcely as much as an 'if you please,' after frightening the wits out of the other girls, so that they can't turn out a room by themselves or walk alone down the stairs for fear of treading on half-frozen toads or hearing it run along the passages at night, all I can say is that it's no place for me. So I must ask you, Mr. Borlsover, sir, to find a new housekeeper that has no objection to large and lonely houses, which some people do say, not that I believe them for a minute, my poor mother always having been a Wesleyan, are haunted.

"Yours faithfully,
Elizabeth Merrit.

"P. S. — I should be obliged if you would give my respects to Mr. Saunders. I hope that he won't run no risks with his cold."

"Saunders," said Eustace, "you've always had a wonderful way with you in dealing with servants. You mustn't let poor old Merrit go."

"Of course she shan't go," said Saunders. "She's probably only angling for a rise in salary. I'll write to her this morning."

"No; there's nothing like a personal interview. We've had enough of town. We'll go back to-morrow, and you must work your cold for all it's worth. Don't forget that it's got on to the chest, and will require weeks of feeding up and nursing."

"All right. I think I can manage Mrs. Merrit."

But Mrs. Merrit was more obstinate than he had thought. She was very sorry to hear of Mr. Saunders's cold, and how he lay awake all night in London coughing; very sorry indeed. She'd change his room for him gladly, and get the south room aired. And wouldn't he have a hot basin of bread and milk last thing at night? But she was afraid that she would have to leave at the end of the month.

"Try her with an increase of salary," was the advice of Eustace.

It was no use. Mrs. Merrit was obdurate, though she knew of a Mrs. Handyside who had been housekeeper to Lord Gargrave, who might be glad to come at the salary mentioned.

"What's the matter with the servants, Morton?" asked Eustace that evening when he brought the coffee into the library. "What's all this about Mrs. Merrit wanting to leave?"

"If you please, sir, I was going to mention it myself. I have a confession to make, sir. When I found your note asking me to open that desk and take out the box with the rat, I broke the lock as you told me, and was glad to do it, because I could hear the animal in the box making a great noise, and I thought it wanted food. So I took out the box, sir, and got a cage and was going to transfer it, when the animal got away."

"What in the world are you talking about? I never wrote any such note."

"Excuse me, sir, it was the note I picked up here on the floor on the day you and Mr. Saunders left. I have it in my pocket now."

It certainly seemed to be in Eustace's handwriting. It was written in pencil, and began somewhat abruptly.

"Get a hammer, Morton," he read, "or some other tool, and break open the lock in the old desk in the library. Take out the box that is inside. You need not do anything else. The lid is already open. Eustace Borlsover."

"And you opened the desk?"

"Yes, sir; and as I was getting the cage ready the animal hopped out."

"What animal?"

"The animal inside the box, sir."

"What did it look like?"

"Well, sir, I couldn't tell you," said Morton nervously; "my back was turned, and it was half-way down the room when I looked up."

"What was its colour?" asked Saunders; "black?"

"Oh, no, sir, a grayish white. It crept along in a very funny way, sir. I don't think it had a tail."

"What did you do then?"

"I tried to catch it, but it was no use. So I set the rat-traps and kept the library shut. Then that girl Emma Laidlaw left the door open when she was cleaning, and I think it must have escaped."

"And you think it was the animal that's been frightening the maids?"

"Well, no, sir, not quite. They said it was — you'll excuse me, sir — a hand that they saw. Emma trod on it once at the bottom of the stairs. She thought then it was a half-frozen toad, only white. And then Parfit was washing up the dishes in the scullery. She wasn't thinking about anything in particular. It was close on dusk. She took her hands out of the water and was drying them absentminded like on the roller towel, when she found that she was drying someone else's hand as well, only colder than hers."

"What nonsense!" exclaimed Saunders.

"Exactly, sir; that's what I told her; but we couldn't get her to stop."

"You don't believe all this?" said Eustace, turning suddenly towards the butler.

"Me, sir? Oh, no, sir! I've not seen anything."

"Nor heard anything?"

"Well, sir, if you must know, the bells do ring at odd times, and there's nobody there when we go; and when we go round to draw the blinds of a night, as often as not somebody's been there before us. But as I says to Mrs. Merrit, a young monkey might do wonderful things, and we all know that Mr. Borlsover has had some strange animals about the place."

"Very well, Morton, that will do."

"What do you make of it?" asked Saunders when they were alone. "I mean of the letter he said you wrote."

"Oh, that's simple enough," said Eustace. "See the paper it's written on? I stopped using that years ago, but there were a few odd sheets and envelopes left in the old desk. We never fastened up the lid of the box before locking it in. The hand got out, found a pencil, wrote this note, and shoved it through the crack on to the floor where Morton found it. That's plain as daylight."

"But the hand couldn't write?"

"Couldn't it? You've not seen it do the things I've seen," and he told Saunders more of what had happened at Eastbourne.

"Well," said Saunders, "in that case we have at least an explanation of the legacy. It was the hand which wrote unknown to your uncle that letter to your solicitor, bequeathing itself to you. Your uncle had no more to do with that request than I. In fact, it would seem that he had some idea of this automatic writing, and feared it."

"Then if it's not my uncle, what is it?"

"I suppose some people might say that a disembodied spirit had got your uncle to educate and prepare a little body for it. Now it's got into that little body and is off on its own."

"Well, what are we to do?"

"We'll keep our eyes open," said Saunders, "and try to catch it. If we can't do that, we shall have to wait till the bally clockwork runs down. After all, if it's flesh and blood, it can't live forever."

For two days nothing happened. Then Saunders saw it sliding down the banister in the hall. He was taken unawares, and lost a full second before he started in pursuit, only to find that the thing had escaped him. Three days later, Eustace, writing alone in the library at night, saw it sitting on an open book at the other end of the room. The fingers crept over the page, feeling the print as if it were reading; but before he had time to get up from his seat, it had taken the alarm and was pulling itself up the curtains. Eustace watched it grimly as it hung on to the cornice with three fingers, flicking thumb and forefinger at him in an expression of scornful derision.

"I know what I'll do," he said. "If I only get it into the open I'll set the dogs on to it."

He spoke to Saunders of the suggestion.

"It's a jolly good idea," he said; "only we won't wait till we find it out of doors. We'll get the dogs. There are the two terriers and the underkeeper's Irish mongrel that's on to rats like a flash. Your spaniel has not got spirit enough for this sort of game." They brought the dogs into the house, and the keeper's Irish mongrel chewed up the slippers, and the terriers tripped up Morton as he waited at table; but all three were welcome. Even false security is better than no security at all.

For a fortnight nothing happened. Then the hand was caught, not by the dogs, but by Mrs. Merrit's gray parrot. The bird was in the habit of periodically removing the pins that kept its seed and water tins in place, and of escaping through the holes in the side of the cage. When once at liberty Peter would show no inclination to return, and would often be about the house for days. Now, after six consecutive weeks of captivity, Peter had again discovered a new means of unloosing his bolts and was at large, exploring the tapestried forests of the curtains and singing songs in praise of liberty from cornice and picture rail.

"It's no use your trying to catch him," said Eustace to Mrs. Merrit, as she came into the study one afternoon toward dusk with a step-ladder. "You'd much better leave Peter alone. Starve him into surrender, Mrs. Merrit, and don't leave bananas and seed about for him to peck at when he fancies he's hungry. You're far too soft-hearted."

"Well, sir, I see he's right out of reach now on that picture rail, so if you wouldn't mind closing the door, sir, when you leave the room, I'll bring his cage in tonight and put some meat inside it. He's that fond of meat, though it does make him pull out his feathers to suck the quills. They *do* say that if you cook — "

"Never mind, Mrs. Merrit," said Eustace, who was busy writing. "That will do; I'll keep an eye on the bird."

There was silence in the room, unbroken but for the continuous whisper of his pen.

"Scratch poor Peter," said the bird. "Scratch poor old Peter!"

"Be quiet, you beastly bird!"

"Poor old Peter! Scratch poor Peter, do."

"I'm more likely to wring your neck if I get hold of you." He looked up at the picture rail, and there was the hand holding on to a hook with three fingers, and slowly scratching the head of the parrot with the fourth. Eustace ran to the bell and pressed it hard; then across to the window, which he closed with a bang. Frightened by the noise the parrot shook its wings preparatory to flight, and as it did so the fingers of the hand got hold of it by the throat. There was a shrill scream from Peter as he fluttered across the room, wheeling round in circles that ever descended, borne down under the weight that clung to him. The bird dropped at last quite suddenly, and Eustace saw fingers and feathers rolled into an inextricable mass on the floor. The struggle abruptly ceased as finger and thumb squeezed the neck; the bird's eyes rolled up to show the whites, and there was a faint, half-choked gurgle. But before the fingers had time to loose their hold, Eustace had them in his own.

"Send Mr. Saunders here at once," he said to the maid who came in answer to the bell. "Tell him I want him immediately."

Then he went with the hand to the fire. There was a ragged gash across the back where the bird's beak had torn it, but no blood oozed from the wound. He noticed with disgust that the nails had grown long and discoloured.

"I'll burn the beastly thing," he said. But he could not burn it. He tried to throw it into the flames, but his own hands, as if restrained by some old primitive feeling, would not let him. And so Saunders found him, pale and irresolute, with the hand still clasped tightly in his fingers.

"I've got it at last," he said in a tone of triumph.

"Good; let's have a look at it."

"Not when it's loose. Get me some nails and a hammer and a board of some sort."

"Can you hold it all right?"

"Yes, the thing's quite limp; tired out with throttling poor old Peter, I should say."

"And now," said Saunders when he returned with the things, "what are we going to do?"

"Drive a nail through it first, so that it can't get away; then we can take our time over examining it."

"Do it yourself," said Saunders. "I don't mind helping you with guinea-pigs occasionally when there's something to be learned; partly because I don't fear a guinea-pig's revenge. This thing's different."

"All right, you miserable skunk. I won't forget the way you've stood by me."

He took up a nail, and before Saunders had realized what he was doing had driven it through the hand, deep into the board.

"Oh, my aunt," he giggled hysterically, "look at it

now," for the hand was writhing in agonized contortions, squirming and wriggling upon the nail like a worm upon the hook.

"Well," said Saunders, "you've done it now. I'll leave you to examine it."

"Don't go, in heaven's name. Cover it up, man, cover it up! Shove a cloth over it! Here!" and he pulled off the antimacassar from the back of a chair and wrapped the board in it. "Now get the keys from my pocket and open the safe. Chuck the other things out. Oh, Lord, it's getting itself into frightful knots! and open it quick!" He threw the thing in and banged the door.

"We'll keep it there till it dies," he said. "May I burn in hell if I ever open the door of that safe again."

*****

Mrs. Merrit departed at the end of the month. Her successor certainly was more successful in the management of the servants. Early in her rule she declared that she would stand no nonsense, and gossip soon withered and died. Eustace Borlsover went back to his old way of life. Old habits crept over and covered his new experience. He was if anything, less morose, and showed a greater inclination to take his natural part in country society.

"I shouldn't be surprised if he marries one of these days," said Saunders. "Well, I'm in no hurry for such an event. I know Eustace far too well for the future Mrs. Borlsover to like me. It will be the same old story again: a long friendship slowly made — marriage — and a long friendship quickly forgotten."

IV

But Eustace Borlsover did not follow the advice of his uncle and marry. He was too fond of old slippers and tobacco. The cooking, too, under Mrs. Handyside's management was excellent, and she seemed, too, to have a heaven-sent faculty in knowing when to stop dusting.

Little by little the old life resumed its old power. Then came the burglary. The men, it was said, broke into the house by way of the conservatory. It was really little more than an attempt, for they only succeeded in carrying away a few pieces of plate from the pantry. The safe in the study was certainly found open and empty, but, as Mr. Borlsover informed the police inspector, he had kept nothing of value in it during the last six months.

"Then you're lucky in getting off so easily, sir," the man replied. "By the way they have gone about their business, I should say they were experienced cracksmen. They must have caught the alarm when they were just beginning their evening's work."

"Yes," said Eustace, "I suppose I am lucky."

"I've no doubt," said the inspector, "that we shall be able to trace the men. I've said that they must have been old hands at the game. The way they got in and opened the safe shows that. But there's one little thing that puzzles me. One of them was careless enough not to wear gloves, and I'm bothered if I know what he was trying to do. I've traced his finger-marks on the new varnish on the window sashes in every one of the downstairs rooms. They are very distinctive ones too."

"Right hand or left, or both?" asked Eustace.

"Oh, right every time. That's the funny thing. He

must have been a foolhardy fellow, and I rather think it was him that wrote that." He took out a slip of paper from his pocket. "That's what he wrote, sir. 'I've got out, Eustace Borlsover, but I'll be back before long.' Some jail bird just escaped, I suppose. It will make it all the easier for us to trace him. Do you know the writing, sir?"

"No," said Eustace; "it's not the writing of any one I know."

"I'm not going to stay here any longer," said Eustace to Saunders at luncheon. "I've got on far better during the last six months than ever I expected, but I'm not going to run the risk of seeing that thing again. I shall go up to town this afternoon. Get Morton to put my things together, and join me with the car at Brighton on the day after to-morrow. And bring the proofs of those two papers with you. We'll run over them together."

"How long are you going to be away?"

"I can't say for certain, but be prepared to stay for some time. We've stuck to work pretty closely through the summer, and I for one need a holiday. I'll engage the rooms at Brighton. You'll find it best to break the journey at Hitchin. I'll wire to you there at the Crown to tell you the Brighton address."

The house he chose at Brighton was in a terrace. He had been there before. It was kept by his old college gyp, a man of discreet silence, who was admirably partnered by an excellent cook. The rooms were on the first floor. The two bedrooms were at the back, and opened out of each other. "Saunders can have the smaller one, though it is the only one with a fireplace," he said. "I'll stick to the larger of the two, since it's got a bathroom adjoining. I wonder what time he'll arrive with the car."

Saunders came about seven, cold and cross and dirty. "We'll light the fire in the dining-room," said Eustace, "and get Prince to unpack some of the things while we are at dinner. What were the roads like?"

"Rotten; swimming with mud, and a beastly cold wind against us all day. And this is July. Dear old England!"

"Yes," said Eustace, "I think we might do worse than leave dear old England for a few months."

They turned in soon after twelve.

"You oughtn't to feel cold, Saunders," said Eustace, "when you can afford to sport a great cat-skin lined coat like this. You do yourself very well, all things considered. Look at those gloves, for instance. Who could possibly feel cold when wearing them?"

"They are far too clumsy though for driving. Try them on and see," and he tossed them through the door on to Eustace's bed, and went on with his unpacking. A minute later he heard a shrill cry of terror. "Oh, Lord," he heard, "it's in the glove! Quick, Saunders, quick!" Then came a smacking thud. Eustace had thrown it from him. "I've chucked it into the bathroom," he gasped, "it's hit the wall and fallen into the bath. Come now if you want to help." Saunders, with a lighted candle in his hand, looked over the edge of the bath. There it was, old and maimed, dumb and blind, with a ragged hole in the middle, crawling, staggering, trying to creep up the slippery sides, only to fall back helpless.

"Stay there," said Saunders. "I'll empty a collar box or something, and we'll jam it in. It can't get out while I'm away."

"Yes, it can," shouted Eustace. "It's getting out now. It's climbing up the plug chain. No, you brute, you filthy brute, you don't! Come back, Saunders, it's getting away from me. I can't hold it; it's all slippery. Curse its claw! Shut the window, you idiot! The top too, as well as the bottom. You utter idiot! It's got out!" There was the sound of something dropping on to the hard flagstones below, and Eustace fell back fainting.

*****

For a fortnight he was ill.

"I don't know what to make of it," the doctor said to Saunders. "I can only suppose that Mr. Borlsover has suffered some great emotional shock. You had better let me send someone to help you nurse him. And by all means indulge that whim of his never to be left alone in the dark. I would keep a light burning all night if I were you. But he *must* have more fresh air. It's perfectly absurd — this hatred of open windows."

Eustace, however, would have no one with him but Saunders. "I don't want the other men," he said. "They'd smuggle it in somehow. I know they would."

"Don't worry about it, old chap. This sort of thing can't go on indefinitely. You know I saw it this time as well as you. It wasn't half so active. It won't go on living much longer, especially after that fall. I heard it hit the flags myself. As soon as you're a bit stronger we'll leave this place; not bag and baggage, but with only the clothes on our backs, so that it won't be able to hide anywhere. We'll escape it that way. We won't give any address, and we won't have any parcels sent after us. Cheer up, Eustace! You'll be well enough to leave in a day or two. The doctor says I can take you out in a chair to-morrow."

"What have I done?" asked Eustace. "Why does it come after me? I'm no worse than other men. I'm no worse than you, Saunders; you know I'm not. It was you who were at the bottom of that dirty business in San Diego, and that was fifteen years ago."

"It's not that, of course," said Saunders. "We are in the twentieth century, and even the parsons have dropped the idea of your old sins finding you out. Before you caught the hand in the library it was filled with pure malevolence — to you and all mankind. After you spiked it through with that nail it naturally forgot about other people, and concentrated its attention on you. It was shut up in that safe, you know, for nearly six months. That gives plenty of time for thinking of revenge."

Eustace Borlsover would not leave his room, but he thought that there might be something in Saunders's suggestion to leave Brighton without notice. He began rapidly to regain his strength.

"We'll go on the first of September," he said.

*****

The evening of August 31st was oppressively warm. Though at midday the windows had been wide open, they had been shut an hour or so before dusk. Mrs. Prince had long since ceased to wonder at the strange habits of the gentlemen on the first floor. Soon after their arrival she had been told to take down the heavy window curtains in the two bedrooms, and day by day the rooms had seemed to grow more bare. Nothing was left lying about.

"Mr. Borlsover doesn't like to have any place where dirt can collect," Saunders had said as an excuse. "He likes to see into all the corners of the room."

"Couldn't I open the window just a little?" he said to Eustace that evening. "We're simply roasting in here, you know."

"No, leave well alone. We're not a couple of boarding-school misses fresh from a course of hygiene lectures. Get the chessboard out."

They sat down and played. At ten o'clock Mrs. Prince came to the door with a note. "I am sorry I didn't bring it before," she said, "but it was left in the letter-box."

"Open it, Saunders, and see if it wants answering."

It was very brief. There was neither address nor signature.

"Will eleven o'clock to-night be suitable for our last appointment?"

"Who is it from?" asked Borlsover.

"It was meant for me," said Saunders. "There's no answer, Mrs. Prince," and he put the paper into his pocket. "A dunning letter from a tailor; I suppose he must have got wind of our leaving."

It was a clever lie, and Eustace asked no more questions. They went on with their game.

On the landing outside Saunders could hear the grandfather's clock whispering the seconds, blurting out the quarter-hours.

"Check!" said Eustace. The clock struck eleven. At the same time there was a gentle knocking on the door; it seemed to come from the bottom panel.

"Who's there?" asked Eustace.

There was no answer.

"Mrs. Prince, is that you?"

"She is up above," said Saunders; "I can hear her walking about the room."

"Then lock the door; bolt it too. Your move, Saunders."

While Saunders sat with his eyes on the chess-board, Eustace walked over to the window and examined the fastenings. He did the same in Saunders's room and the bathroom. There were no doors between the three rooms, or he would have shut and locked them too.

"Now, Saunders," he said, "don't stay all night over your move. I've had time to smoke one cigarette already. It's bad to keep an invalid waiting. There's only one possible thing for you to do. What was that?"

"The ivy blowing against the window. There, it's your move now, Eustace."

"It wasn't the ivy, you idiot. It was someone tapping at the window," and he pulled up the blind. On the outer side of the window, clinging to the sash, was the hand.

"What is it that it's holding?"

"It's a pocket-knife. It's going to try to open the window by pushing back the fastener with the blade."

"Well, let it try," said Eustace. "Those fasteners screw down; they can't be opened that way. Anyhow, we'll close the shutters. It's your move, Saunders. I've played."

But Saunders found it impossible to fix his attention on the game. He could not understand Eustace who seemed all at once to have lost his fear. "What do you say to some wine?" he asked. "You seem to be taking things coolly, but I don't mind confessing that I'm in a blessed funk."

"You've no need to be. There's nothing supernatural about that hand, Saunders. I mean it seems to be governed by the laws of time and space. It's not the sort of thing that vanishes into thin air or slides through oaken doors. And since that's so, I defy it to get in here. We'll leave the place in the morning. I for one have bottomed the depths of fear. Fill your glass, man! The windows are all shuttered, the door is locked and bolted. Pledge me my uncle Adrian! Drink, man! What are you waiting for?"

Saunders was standing with his glass half raised. "It can get in," he said hoarsely; "it can get in! We've forgotten. There's the fireplace in my bedroom. It will come down the chimney."

"Quick!" said Eustace, as he rushed into the other room; "we haven't a minute to lose. What can we do? Light the fire, Saunders. Give me a match, quick!"

"They must be all in the other room. I'll get them."

"Hurry, man, for goodness' sake! Look in the bookcase! Look in the bathroom! Here, come and stand here; I'll look."

"Be quick!" shouted Saunders. "I can hear something!"

"Then plug a sheet from your bed up the chimney. No, here's a match." He had found one at last that had slipped into a crack in the floor.

"Is the fire laid? Good, but it may not burn. I know — the oil from that old reading-lamp and this cotton-wool. Now the match, quick! Pull the sheet away, you fool! We don't want it now."

There was a great roar from the grate as the flames shot up. Saunders had been a fraction of a second too late with the sheet. The oil had fallen on to it. It, too, was burning.

"The whole place will be on fire!" cried Eustace, as he tried to beat out the flames with a blanket. "It's no good! I can't manage it. You must open the door, Saunders, and get help."

Saunders ran to the door and fumbled with the bolts. The key was stiff in the lock.

"Hurry!" shouted Eustace; "the whole place is ablaze!"

The key turned in the lock at last. For half a second Saunders stopped to look back. Afterwards he could never be quite sure as to what he had seen, but at the time he thought that something black and charred was creeping slowly, very slowly, from the mass of flames toward Eustace Borlsover. For a moment he thought of returning to his friend, but the noise and the smell of the burning sent him running down the passage crying, "Fire! Fire!" He rushed to the telephone to summon help, and then back to the bathroom — he should have thought of that before — for water. As he burst open the bedroom door there came a scream of terror which ended suddenly, and then the sound of a heavy fall.

*****

This is the story which I heard on successive Saturday evenings from the senior mathematical master at a second-rate suburban school. For Saunders has had to earn a living in a way which other men might reckon less congenial than his old manner of life. I had mentioned by chance the name of Adrian Borlsover, and wondered at the time why he changed the conversation with such unusual abruptness. A week later, Saunders began to tell me something of his own history — sordid enough, though shielded with a reserve I could well understand, for it had to cover not only his failings but those of a dead friend. Of the final tragedy he was at first especially loath to speak, and it was only gradually that I was able to piece together the narrative of the preceding pages. Saunders was reluctant to draw any conclusions. At one time he thought that the fingered beast had been animated by the spirit of Sigismund Borlsover, a sinister eighteenth-century ancestor, who, according to legend, built and worshipped in the ugly pagan temple that overlooked the lake. At another time Saunders believed the spirit to belong to a man whom Eustace had once employed as a laboratory assistant, "a black-haired spiteful little brute," he said, "who died cursing his doctor because the fellow couldn't help him to live to settle some paltry score with Borlsover."

From the point of view of direct contemporary evidence, Saunders's story is practically uncorroborated. All the letters mentioned in the narrative were destroyed, with the exception of the last note which Eustace received, or rather which he would have received had not Saunders intercepted it. That I have seen myself. The handwriting was thin and shaky, the handwriting of an old man. I remember the Greek "e" was used in "appointment." A little thing that amused me at the time was that Saunders seemed to keep the note pressed between the pages of his Bible.

I had seen Adrian Borlsover once. Saunders, I learnt to know well. It was by chance, however, and not by design, that I met a third person of the story, Morton the butler. Saunders and I were walking in the Zoological Gardens one Sunday afternoon, when he called my attention to an old man who was standing before the door of the reptile house.

"Why, Morton!" he said, clapping him on the back. "How is the world treating you?"

"Poorly, Mr. Saunders," said the old fellow, though his face lighted up at the greeting. "The winters drag terribly nowadays. There don't seem no summers or springs."

"You haven't found what you were looking for, I suppose?"

"No, sir, not yet; but I shall some day. I always told them that Mr. Borlsover kept some queer animals."

"And what is he looking for?" I asked, when we had parted from him.

"A beast with five fingers," said Saunders. "This afternoon, since he has been in the reptile house, I suppose it will be a reptile with a hand. Next week it will be a monkey with practically no body. The poor old chap is a born materialist.

"It's a queer coincidence, by the way, that you should have known Adrian Borlsover and that you should have received a blessing at his hand. Has it brought you any luck?"

"No," I answered slowly, as I looked back over a life of inconspicuous failure, "I don't think it has. It was his right hand, you know."

VI. Sister Maddelena. – Ralph Adams Cram

Across the valley of the Oreto from Monreale, on the slopes of the mountains just above the little village of Parco, lies the old convent of Sta. Catarina. From the cloister terrace at Monreale you can see its pale walls and the slim campanile of its chapel rising from the crowded citron and mulberry orchards that flourish, rank and wild, no longer cared for by pious and loving hands. From the rough road that climbs the mountains to Assunto, the convent is invisible, a gnarled and ragged olive grove intervening, and a spur of cliffs as well, while from Palermo one sees only the speck of white, flashing in the sun, indistinguishable from the many similar gleams of desert monastery or pauper village.

Partly because of this seclusion, partly by reason of its extreme beauty, partly, it may be, because the present owners are more than charming and gracious in their pressing hospitality, Sta. Catarina seems to preserve an element of the poetic, almost magical; and as I drove with the Cavaliere Valguanera one evening in March out of Palermo, along the garden valley of the Oreto, then up the mountain side where the warm light of the spring sunset swept across from Monreale, lying golden and mellow on the luxuriant growth of figs, and olives, and orange-trees, and fantastic cacti, and so up to where the path of the convent swung off to the right round a dizzy point of cliff that reached out gaunt and gray from the olives below, – as I drove thus in the balmy air, and saw of a sudden a vision of creamy walls and orange roof, draped in fantastic festoons of roses, with a single curving palm-tree stuck black and feathery against the gold sunset, it is hardly to be wondered at that I should slip into a mood of visionary enjoyment, looking for a time on the whole thing as the misty phantasm of a summer dream.

The Cavaliere had introduced himself to us, — Tom Rendel and me, — one morning soon after we reached Palermo, when, in the first bewilderment of architects in this paradise of art and colour, we were working nobly at our sketches in that dream of delight, the Capella Palatina. He was himself an amateur archæologist, he told us, and passionately devoted to his island; so he felt impelled to speak to anyone whom he saw appreciating the almost — and in a way fortunately — unknown beauties of Palermo. In a little time we were fully acquainted, and talking like the oldest friends. Of course he knew acquaintances of Rendel's, — someone always does: this time they were officers on the tubby U. S. S. *Quinebaug*, that, during the summer of 1888, was trying to uphold the maritime honour of the United States in European waters. Luckily for us, one of the officers was a kind of cousin of Rendel's, and came from Baltimore as well, so, as he had visited at the Cavaliere's place, we were soon invited to do the same. It was in this way that, with the luck that attends Rendel wherever he goes, we came to see something of domestic life in Italy, and that I found myself involved in another of those adventures for which I naturally sought so little.

I wonder if there is any other place in Sicily so faultless as Sta. Catarina? Taormina is a paradise, an epitome of all that is beautiful in Italy, — Venice excepted. Girgenti is a solemn epic, with its golden temples between the sea and hills. Cefalú is wild and strange, and Monreale a vision out of a fairy tale; but Sta. Catarina! —

Fancy a convent of creamy stone and rose red brick perched on a ledge of rock midway between earth and heaven, the cliff falling almost sheer to the valley two hundred feet and more, the mountain rising behind straight toward the sky; all the rocks covered with cactus and dwarf fig-trees, the convent draped in smothering roses, and in front a terrace with a fountain in the midst; and then — nothing — between you and the sapphire sea, six miles away. Below stretches the Eden valley, the Concha d'Oro, gold-green fig orchards alternating with smoke-blue olives, the mountains rising on either hand and sinking undulously away toward the bay where, like a magic city of ivory and nacre, Palermo lies guarded by the twin mountains, Monte Pelligrino and Capo Zafferano, arid rocks like dull amethysts, rose in sunlight, violet in shadow: lions couchant, guarding the sleeping town.

Seen as we saw it for the first time that hot evening in March, with the golden lambent light pouring down through the valley, making it in verity a "shell of gold," sitting in Indian chairs on the terrace, with the perfume of roses and jasmines all around us, the valley of the Oreto, Palermo, Sta. Catarina, Monreale, — all were but parts of a dreamy vision, like the heavenly city of Sir Percivale, to attain which he passed across the golden bridge that burned after him as he vanished in the intolerable light of the Beatific Vision.

It was all so unreal, so phantasmal, that I was not surprised in the least when, late in the evening after the ladies had gone to their rooms, and the Cavaliere, Tom, and I were stretched out in chairs on the terrace, smoking lazily under the multitudinous stars, the Cavaliere said, "There is something I really must tell you both before you go to bed, so that you may be spared any unnecessary alarm."

"You are going to say that the place is haunted," said Rendel, feeling vaguely on the floor beside him for his glass of Amaro: "thank you; it is all it needs."

The Cavaliere smiled a little: "Yes, that is just it. Sta. Catarina is really haunted; and much as my reason revolts against the idea as superstitious and savouring of priestcraft, yet I must acknowledge I see no way of avoiding the admission. I do not presume to offer any explanations, I only state the fact; and the fact is that to-night one or other of you will, in all human — or unhuman — probability, receive a visit from Sister Maddelena. You need not be in the least afraid, the apparition is perfectly gentle and harmless; and, moreover, having seen it once, you will never see it again. No one sees the ghost, or whatever it is, but once, and that usually the first night he spends in the house. I myself saw the thing eight — nine years ago, when I first bought the place from the Marchese di Muxaro; all my people have seen it, nearly all my guests, so I think you may as well be prepared."

"Then tell us what to expect," I said; "what kind of a ghost is this nocturnal visitor?"

"It is simple enough. Some time to-night you will suddenly awake and see before you a Carmelite nun who will look fixedly at you, say distinctly and very sadly, 'I cannot sleep,' and then vanish. That is all, it is hardly worth speaking of, only some people are terribly frightened if they are visited unwarned by strange apparitions; so I tell you this that you may be prepared."

"This was a Carmelite convent, then?" I said.

"Yes; it was suppressed after the unification of Italy, and given to the House of Muxaro; but the family died out, and I bought it. There is a story about the ghostly nun, who was only a novice, and even that unwillingly, which gives an interest to an otherwise very commonplace and uninteresting ghost."

"I beg that you will tell it us," cried Rendel.

"There is a storm coming," I added. "See, the lightning is flashing already up among the mountains at the head of the valley; if the story is tragic, as it must be, now is just the time for it. You will tell it, will you not?"

The Cavaliere smiled that slow, cryptic smile of his that was so unfathomable.

"As you say, there is a shower coming, and as we have fierce tempests here, we might not sleep; so perhaps we may as well sit up a little longer, and I will tell you the story."

The air was utterly still, hot and oppressive; the rich, sick odour of the oranges just bursting into bloom came up from the valley in a gently rising tide. The sky, thick with stars, seemed mirrored in the rich foliage below, so numerous were the glow-worms under the still trees, and the fireflies that gleamed in the hot air. Lightning flashed fitfully from the darkening west; but as yet no thunder broke the heavy silence.

The Cavaliere lighted another cigar, and pulled a cushion under his head so that he could look down to the distant lights of the city. "This is the story," he said.

"Once upon a time, late in the last century, the Duca di Castiglione was attached to the court of Charles III., King of the Two Sicilies, down at Palermo. They tell me he was very ambitious, and, not content with marrying his son to one of the ladies of the House of Tuscany, had betrothed his only daughter, Rosalia, to Prince Antonio, a cousin of the king. His whole life was wrapped up in the fame of his family, and he quite forgot all domestic affection in his madness for dynastic glory. His son was a worthy scion, cold and proud; but Rosalia was, according to legend, utterly the reverse, — a passionate, beautiful girl, wilful and headstrong, and careless of her family and the world.

"The time had nearly come for her to marry Prince Antonio, a typical *roué* of the Spanish court, when, through the treachery of a servant, the Duke discovered that his daughter was in love with a young military officer whose name I don't remember, and that an elopement had been planned to take place the next night. The fury and dismay of the old autocrat passed belief; he saw in a flash the downfall of all his hopes of family aggrandizement through union with the royal house, and, knowing well the spirit of his daughter, despaired of ever bringing her to subjection. Nevertheless, he attacked her unmercifully, and, by bullying and threats, by imprisonment, and even bodily chastisement, he tried to break her spirit and bend her to his indomitable will. Through his power at court he had the lover sent away to the mainland, and for more than a year he held his daughter closely imprisoned in his palace on the Toledo, — that one, you may remember, on the right, just beyond the Via del Collegio dei Gesuiti, with the beautiful ironwork grilles at all the windows, and the painted frieze. But nothing could move her, nothing bend her stubborn will; and at last, furious at the girl he could not govern, Castiglione sent her to this convent, then one of the few houses of barefoot Carmelite nuns in Italy. He stipulated that she should take the name of Maddelena, that he should never hear of her again, and that she should be held an absolute prisoner in this conventual castle.

"Rosalia — or Sister Maddelena, as she was now — believed her lover dead, for her father had given her good proofs of this, and she believed him; nevertheless she refused to marry another, and seized upon the convent life as a blessed relief from the tyranny of her maniacal father.

"She lived here for four or five years; her name was forgotten at court and in her father's palace. Rosalia di Castiglione was dead, and only Sister Maddelena lived, a Carmelite nun, in her place.

"In 1798 Ferdinand IV. found himself driven from his throne on the mainland, his kingdom divided, and he himself forced to flee to Sicily. With him came the lover of the dead Rosalia, now high in military honour. He on his part had thought Rosalia dead, and it was only by accident that he found that she still lived, a Carmelite nun. Then began the second act of the romance that until then had been only sadly commonplace, but now became dark and tragic. Michele — Michele Biscari, — that was his name; I remember now — haunted the region of the convent, striving to communicate with Sister Maddelena; and at last, from the cliffs over us, up there among the citrons — you will see by the next flash of lightning — he saw her in the great cloister, recognized her in her white habit, found her the same dark and splendid beauty of six years before, only made more beautiful by her white habit and her rigid life. By and by he found a day when she was alone, and tossed a ring to her as she stood in the midst of the cloister. She looked up, saw him, and from that moment lived only to love him in life as she had loved his memory in the death she had thought had overtaken him.

"With the utmost craft they arranged their plans together. They could not speak, for a word would have aroused the other inmates of the convent. They could make signs only when Sister Maddelena was alone. Michele could throw notes to her from the cliff, — a feat demanding a strong arm, as you will see, if you measure the distance with your eye, — and she could drop replies from the window over the cliff, which he picked up at the bottom. Finally he succeeded in casting into the cloister a coil of light rope. The girl fastened it to the bars of one of the windows, and — so great is the madness of love — Biscari actually climbed the rope from the valley to the window of the cell, a distance of almost two hundred feet, with but three little craggy resting-places in all that height. For nearly a month these nocturnal visits were undiscovered, and Michele had almost completed his arrangements for carrying the girl from Sta. Catarina and away to Spain, when unfortunately one of the sisters, suspecting some mystery, from the changed face of Sister Maddelena, began investigating, and at length discovered the rope neatly coiled up by the nun's window, and hidden under some clinging vines. She instantly told the Mother Superior; and together they watched from a window in the crypt of the chapel, — the only place, as you will see to-morrow, from which one could see the window of Sister Maddelena's cell. They saw the figure of Michele daringly ascending the slim rope; watched hour after hour, the Sister remaining while the Superior went to say the hours in the chapel, at each of which Sister Maddelena was present; and at last, at prime, just as the sun was rising, they saw the figure slip down the rope, watched the rope drawn up and concealed, and knew that Sister Maddelena was in their hands for vengeance and punishment, — a criminal.

"The next day, by the order of the Mother Superior, Sister Maddelena was imprisoned in one of the cells under the chapel, charged with her guilt, and commanded to make full and complete confession. But not a word would she say, although they offered her forgiveness if she would tell the name of her lover. At last the Superior told her that after this fashion would they act the coming night: she herself would be placed in the crypt, tied in front of the window, her mouth gagged; that the rope would be lowered, and the lover allowed to approach even to the sill of her window, and at that moment the rope would be cut, and before her eyes her lover would be dashed to death on the ragged cliffs. The plan was feasible, and Sister Maddelena knew that the Mother was perfectly capable of carrying it out. Her stubborn spirit was broken, and in the only way possible she begged for mercy, for the sparing of her lover. The Mother Superior was deaf at first; at last she said, 'It is your life or his. I will spare him on condition that you sacrifice your own life.' Sister Maddelena accepted the terms joyfully, wrote a last farewell to Michele, fastened the note to the rope, and with her own hands cut the rope and saw it fall coiling down to the valley bed far below.

"Then she silently prepared for death; and at midnight, while her lover was wandering, mad with the horror of impotent fear, around the white walls of the convent, Sister Maddelena, for love of Michele, gave up her life. How, was never known. That she was indeed dead was only a suspicion, for when Biscari finally compelled the civil authorities to enter the convent, claiming that murder had been done there, they found no sign. Sister Maddelena had been sent to the parent house of the barefoot Carmelites at Avila in Spain, so the Superior stated, because of her incorrigible contumacy. The old Duke of Castiglione refused to stir hand or foot in the matter, and Michele, after fruitless attempts to prove that the Superior of Sta. Catarina had caused the death, was forced to leave Sicily. He sought in Spain for very long; but no sign of the girl was to be found, and at last he died, exhausted with suffering and sorrow.

"Even the name of Sister Maddelena was forgotten, and it was not until the convents were suppressed, and this house came into the hands of the Muxaros, that her story was remembered. It was then that the ghost began to appear; and, an explanation being necessary, the story, or legend, was obtained from one of the nuns who still lived after the suppression. I think the fact — for it is a fact — of the ghost rather goes to prove that Michele was right, and that poor Rosalia gave her life a sacrifice for love, — whether in accordance with the terms of the legend or not, I cannot say. One or the other of you will probably see her to-night. You might ask her for the facts. Well, that is all the story of Sister Maddelena, known in the world as Rosalia di Castiglione. Do you like it?"

"It is admirable," said Rendel, enthusiastically. "But I fancy I should rather look on it simply as a story, and not as a warning of what is going to happen. I don't much fancy real ghosts myself."

"But the poor Sister is quite harmless"; and Valguanera rose, stretching himself. "My servants say she wants a mass said over her, or something of that kind; but I haven't much love for such priestly hocus-pocus, — I beg your pardon" (turning to me), "I had forgotten that you were a Catholic: forgive my rudeness."

"My dear Cavaliere, I beg you not to apologize. I am sorry you cannot see things as I do; but don't for a moment think I am hypersensitive."

"I have an excuse, — perhaps you will say only an explanation; but I live where I see all the absurdities and corruptions of the Church."

"Perhaps you let the accidents blind you to the essentials; but do not let us quarrel to-night, — see, the storm is close on us. Shall we go in?"

The stars were blotted out through nearly all the sky; low, thunderous clouds, massed at the head of the valley, were sweeping over so close that they seemed to brush the black pines on the mountain above us. To the south and east the storm-clouds had shut down almost to the sea, leaving a space of black sky where the moon in its last quarter was rising just to the left of Monte Pellegrino, — a black silhouette against the pallid moonlight. The rosy lightning flashed almost incessantly, and through the fitful darkness came the sound of bells across the valley, the rushing torrent below, and the dull roar of the approaching rain, with a deep organ-point of solemn thunder through it all.

We fled indoors from the coming tempest, and taking our candles, said "good-night," and sought each his respective room.

My own was in the southern part of the old convent, giving on the terrace we had just quitted, and about over the main doorway. The rushing storm, as it swept down the valley with the swelling torrent beneath, was very fascinating, and after wrapping myself in a dressing-gown I stood for some time by the deeply embrasured window, watching the blazing lightning and the beating rain whirled by fitful gusts of wind around the spurs of the mountains. Gradually the violence of the shower seemed to decrease, and I threw myself down on my bed in the hot air, wondering if I really was to experience the ghostly visit the Cavaliere so confidently predicted.

I had thought out the whole matter to my own satisfaction, and fancied I knew exactly what I should do, in case Sister Maddelena came to visit me. The story touched me: the thought of the poor faithful girl who sacrificed herself for her lover, — himself very likely, quite unworthy, — and who now could never sleep for reason of her unquiet soul, sent out into the storm of eternity without spiritual aid or counsel. I could not sleep; for the still vivid lightning, the crowding thoughts of the dead nun, and the shivering anticipation of my possible visitation, made slumber quite out of the question. No suspicion of sleepiness had visited me, when, perhaps an hour after midnight, came a sudden vivid flash of lightning, and, as my dazzled eyes began to regain the power of sight, I saw her as plainly as in life, — a tall figure, shrouded in the white habit of the Carmelites, her head bent, her hands clasped before her. In another flash of lightning she slowly raised her head and looked at me long and earnestly. She was very beautiful, like the Virgin of Beltraffio in the National Gallery, — more beautiful than I had supposed possible, her deep, passionate eyes very tender and pitiful in their pleading, beseeching glance. I hardly think I was frightened, or even startled, but lay looking steadily at her as she stood in the beating lightning.

Then she breathed, rather than articulated, with a voice that almost brought tears, so infinitely sad and sorrowful was it, "I cannot sleep!" and the liquid eyes grew more pitiful and questioning as bright tears fell from them down the pale dark face.

The figure began to move slowly toward the

door, its eyes fixed on mine with a look that was weary and almost agonized. I leaped from the bed and stood waiting. A look of utter gratitude swept over the face, and, turning, the figure passed through the doorway.

Out into the shadow of the corridor it moved, like a drift of pallid storm-cloud, and I followed, all natural and instinctive fear or nervousness quite blotted out by the part I felt I was to play in giving rest to a tortured soul. The corridors were velvet black; but the pale figure floated before me always, an unerring guide, now but a thin mist on the utter night, now white and clear in the bluish lightning through some window or doorway.

Down the stairway into the lower hall, across the refectory, where the great frescoed Crucifixion flared into sudden clearness under the fitful lightning, out into the silent cloister.

It was very dark. I stumbled along the heaving bricks, now guiding myself by a hand on the whitewashed wall, now by a touch on a column wet with the storm. From all the eaves the rain was dripping on to the pebbles at the foot of the arcade: a pigeon, startled from the capital where it was sleeping, beat its way into the cloister close. Still the white thing drifted before me to the farther side of the court, then along the cloister at right angles, and paused before one of the many doorways that led to the cells.

A sudden blaze of fierce lightning, the last now of the fleeting trail of storm, leaped around us, and in the vivid light I saw the white face turned again with the look of overwhelming desire, of beseeching pathos, that had choked my throat with an involuntary sob when first I saw Sister Maddelena. In the brief interval that ensued after the flash, and before the roaring thunder burst like the crash of battle over the trembling convent, I heard again the sorrowful words, "I cannot sleep," come from the impenetrable darkness. And when the lightning came again, the white figure was gone.

I wandered around the courtyard, searching in vain for Sister Maddelena, even until the moonlight broke through the torn and sweeping fringes of the storm. I tried the door where the white figure vanished: it was locked; but I had found what I sought, and, carefully noting its location, went back to my room, but not to sleep.

In the morning the Cavaliere asked Rendel and me which of us had seen the ghost, and I told him my story; then I asked him to grant me permission to sift the thing to the bottom; and he courteously gave the whole matter into my charge, promising that he would consent to anything.

I could hardly wait to finish breakfast; but no sooner was this done than, forgetting my morning pipe, I started with Rendel and the Cavaliere to investigate.

"I am sure there is nothing in that cell," said Valguanera, when we came in front of the door I had marked. "It is curious that you should have chosen the door of the very cell that tradition assigns to Sister Maddelena; but I have often examined that room myself, and I am sure that there is no chance for anything to be concealed. In fact, I had the floor taken up once, soon after I came here, knowing the room was that of the mysterious Sister, and thinking that there, if anywhere, the monastic crime would have taken place; still, we will go in, if you like."

He unlocked the door, and we entered, one of us, at all events, with a beating heart. The cell was very small, hardly eight feet square. There certainly seemed no opportunity for concealing a body in the tiny place; and although I sounded the floor and walls, all gave a solid, heavy answer, — the unmistakable sound of masonry.

For the innocence of the floor the Cavaliere answered. He had, he said, had it all removed, even to the curving surfaces of the vault below; yet somewhere in this room the body of the murdered girl was concealed, — of this I was certain. But where? There seemed no answer; and I was compelled to give up the search for the moment, somewhat to the amusement of Valguanera, who had watched curiously to see if I could solve the mystery.

But I could not forget the subject, and toward noon started on another tour of investigation. I procured the keys from the Cavaliere, and examined the cells adjoining; they were apparently the same, each with its window opposite the door, and nothing — Stay, were they the same? I hastened into the suspected cell; it was as I thought: this cell, being on the corner, could have had two windows, yet only one was visible, and that to the left, at right angles with the doorway. Was it imagination? As I sounded the wall opposite the door, where the other window should be; I fancied that the sound was a trifle less solid and dull. I was becoming excited. I dashed back to the cell on the right, and, forcing open the little window, thrust my head out.

It was found at last! In the smooth surface of the yellow wall was a rough space, following approximately the shape of the other cell windows, not plastered like the rest of the wall, but showing the shapes of bricks through its thick coatings of whitewash. I turned with a gasp of excitement and satisfaction: yes, the embrasure of the wall was deep enough; what a wall it was! — four feet at least, and the opening of the window reached to the floor, though the window itself was hardly three feet square. I felt absolutely certain that the secret was solved, and called the Cavaliere and Rendel, too excited to give them an explanation of my theories.

They must have thought me mad when I suddenly began scraping away at the solid wall in front of the door; but in a few minutes they understood what I was about, for under the coatings of paint and plaster appeared the original bricks; and as my architectural knowledge had led me rightly, the space I had cleared was directly over a vertical joint between firm, workmanlike masonry on one hand, and rough amateurish work on the other, bricks laid anyway, and without order or science.

Rendel seized a pick, and was about to assail the rude wall, when I stopped him.

"Let us be careful," I said; "who knows what we may find?" So we set to work digging out the mortar around a brick at about the level of our eyes.

How hard the mortar had become! But a brick yielded at last, and with trembling fingers I detached it. Darkness within, yet beyond question there was a cavity there, not a solid wall; and with infinite care we removed another brick. Still the hole was too small to admit enough light from the dimly illuminated cell. With a chisel we pried at the sides of a large block of masonry, perhaps eight bricks in size. It moved, and we softly slid it from its bed.

Valguanera, who was standing watching us as

we lowered the bricks to the floor, gave a sudden cry, a cry like that of a frightened woman, — terrible, coming from him. Yet there was cause.

Framed by the ragged opening of the bricks, hardly seen in the dim light, was a face, an ivory image, more beautiful than any antique bust, but drawn and distorted by unspeakable agony: the lovely mouth half open, as though gasping for breath; the eyes cast upward; and below, slim chiselled hands crossed on the breast, but clutching the folds of the white Carmelite habit, torture and agony visible in every tense muscle, fighting against the determination of the rigid pose.

We stood there breathless, staring at the pitiful sight, fascinated, bewitched. So this was the secret. With fiendish ingenuity, the rigid ecclesiastics had blocked up the window, then forced the beautiful creature to stand in the alcove, while with remorseless hands and iron hearts they had shut her into a living tomb. I had read of such things in romance; but to find the verity here, before my eyes —

Steps came down the cloister, and with a simultaneous thought we sprang to the door and closed it behind us. The room was sacred; that awful sight was not for curious eyes. The gardener was coming to ask some trivial question of Valguanera. The Cavaliere cut him short. "Pietro, go down to Parco and ask Padre Stefano to come here at once." (I thanked him with a glance.) "Stay!" He turned to me: "Signore, it is already two o'clock and too late for mass, is it not?"

I nodded.

Valguanera thought a moment, then he said, "Bring two horses; the Signor Americano will go with you, — do you understand?" Then, turning to me,

"You will go, will you not? I think you can explain matters to Padre Stefano better than I."

"Of course I will go, more than gladly." So it happened that after a hasty luncheon I wound down the mountain to Parco, found Padre Stefano, explained my errand to him, found him intensely eager and sympathetic, and by five o'clock had him back at the convent with all that was necessary for the resting of the soul of the dead girl.

In the warm twilight, with the last light of the sunset pouring into the little cell through the window where almost a century ago Rosalia had for the last time said farewell to her lover, we gathered together to speed her tortured soul on its journey, so long delayed. Nothing was omitted; all the needful offices of the Church were said by Padre Stefano, while the light in the window died away, and the flickering flames of the candles carried by two of the acolytes from San Francesco threw fitful flashes of pallid light into the dark recess where the white face had prayed to Heaven for a hundred years.

Finally, the Padre took the asperge from the hands of one of the acolytes, and with a sign of the cross in benediction while he chanted the *Asperges,* gently sprinkled the holy water on the upturned face. Instantly the whole vision crumbled to dust, the face was gone, and where once the candlelight had flickered on the perfect semblance of the girl dead so very long, it now fell only on the rough bricks which closed the window, bricks laid with frozen hearts by pitiless hands.

But our task was not done yet. It had been arranged that Padre Stefano should remain at the convent all night, and that as soon as midnight made it possible he should say the first mass for the repose of the girl's soul. We sat on the terrace talking over the strange events of the last crowded hours, and I noted with satisfaction that the Cavaliere no longer spoke of the Church with that hardness, which had hurt me so often. It is true that the Padre was with us nearly all the time; but not only was Valguanera courteous, he was almost sympathetic; and I wondered if it might not prove that more than one soul benefited by the untoward events of the day.

With the aid of the astonished and delighted servants, and no little help as well from Signora Valguanera, I fitted up the long cold Altar in the chapel, and by midnight we had the gloomy sanctuary beautiful with flowers and candles. It was a curiously solemn service, in the first hour of the new day, in the midst of blazing candles and the thick incense, the odour of the opening orange-blooms drifting up in the fresh morning air, and mingling with the incense smoke and the perfume of flowers within. Many prayers were said that night for the soul of the dead girl, and I think many afterward; for after the benediction I remained for a little time in my place, and when I rose from my knees and went toward the chapel door, I saw a figure kneeling still, and, with a start, recognized the form of the Cavaliere. I smiled with quiet satisfaction and gratitude, and went away softly, content with the chain of events that now seemed finished.

The next day the alcove was again walled up, for the precious dust could not be gathered together for transportation to consecrated ground; so I went down to the little cemetery at Parco for a basket of earth, which we cast in over the ashes of Sister Maddelena.

By and by, when Rendel and I went away, with

great regret, Valguanera came down to Palermo with us; and the last act that we performed in Sicily was assisting him to order a tablet of marble, whereon was carved this simple inscription: —

HERE LIES THE BODY OF
ROSALIA DI CASTIGLIONI,
CALLED
SISTER MADDELENA.
HER SOUL
IS WITH HIM WHO GAVE IT.

To this I added in thought: —

"Let him that is without sin among you cast the first stone."

VII. Thrawn Janet — Robert Louis Stevenson

The Reverend Murdoch Soulis was long minister of the moorland parish of Balweary, in the vale of Dule. A severe, bleak-faced old man, dreadful to his hearers, he dwelt in the last years of his life, without relative or servant or any human company, in the small and lonely manse under the Hanging Shaw. In spite of the iron composure of his features, his eye was wild, scared, and uncertain; and when he dwelt, in private admonitions, on the future of the impenitent, it seemed as if his eye pierced through the storms of time to the terrors of eternity. Many young persons, coming to prepare themselves against the season of the Holy Communion, were dreadfully affected by his talk. He had a sermon on 1st Peter, v. and 8th, "The devil as a roaring lion," on the Sunday after every seventeenth of August, and he was accustomed to surpass himself upon that text both by the appalling nature of the matter and the terror of his bearing in the pulpit. The children were frightened into fits, and the old looked more than usually oracular, and were, all that day, full of those hints that Hamlet deprecated. The manse itself, where it stood by the water of Dule among some thick trees, with the Shaw overhanging it on the one side, and on the other many cold, moorish hill-tops rising toward the sky, had begun, at a very early period of Mr. Soulis's ministry, to be avoided in the dusk hours by all who valued themselves upon their prudence; and guidmen sitting at the clachan alehouse shook their heads together at the thought of passing late by that uncanny neighbourhood. There was one spot, to be more particular, which was regarded with especial awe. The manse stood between the highroad and the water of Dule with a gable to each; its back was toward the kirktown of Balweary, nearly half a mile away; in front of it, a bare garden, hedged with thorn, occupied the land between the river and the road. The house was two stories high, with two large rooms on each. It opened not directly on the garden, but on a causewayed path, or passage, giving on the road on the one hand, and closed on the other by the tall willows and elders that bordered on the stream. And it was this strip of causeway that enjoyed among the young parishioners of Balweary so infamous a reputation. The minister walked there often after dark, sometimes groaning aloud in the instancy of his unspoken prayers; and when he was from home, and the manse door was locked, the more daring schoolboys ventured, with beating hearts, to "follow my leader" across that legendary spot.

This atmosphere of terror, surrounding, as it did, a man of God of spotless character and orthodoxy, was a common cause of wonder and subject of inquiry among the few strangers who were led by chance or business into that unknown, outlying country. But many even of the people of the parish were ignorant of the strange events which had marked the first year of Mr. Soulis's ministrations; and among those who were better informed, some were naturally reticent, and others shy of that particular topic. Now and again, only, one of the older folk would warm into courage over his third tumbler, and recount the cause of the minister's strange and solitary life.

*****

Fifty years syne, when Mr. Soulis cam' first into Ba'weary, he was still a young man — a callant, the folk said — fu' o' book learnin' and grand at the exposition, but, as was natural in sae young a man, wi' nae leevin' experience in religion. The younger sort were greatly taken wi' his gifts and his gab; but auld, concerned, serious men and women were moved even to prayer for the young man, whom they took to be a self-deceiver, and the parish that was like to be sae ill-supplied. It was before the days o' the moderates – weary fa' them; but ill things are like guid – they baith come bit by bit, a pickle at a time; and there were folk even then that said the Lord had left the college professors to their ain devices an' the lads that went to study wi' them wad hae done mair and better sittin' in a peat-bog, like their forbears of the persecution, wi' a Bible under their oxter and a speerit o' prayer in their heart. There was nae doubt, onyway, but that Mr. Soulis had been ower lang at the college. He was careful and troubled for mony things besides the ae thing needful. He had a feck o' books wi' him – mair than had ever been seen before in a' that presbytery; and a sair wark the carrier had wi' them, for they were a' like to have smoored in the Deil's Hag between this and Kilmackerlie. They were books o' divinity, to be sure, or so they ca'd them; but the serious were o' opinion there was little service for sae mony, when the hail o' God's Word would gang in the neuk of a plaid. Then he wad sit half the day and half the nicht forbye, which was scant decent – writin' nae less; and first, they were feared he wad read his sermons; and syne it proved he was writin' a book himsel', which was surely no fittin' for ane of his years and sma' experience.

Onyway it behoved him to get an auld, decent wife to keep the manse for him an' see to his bit denners; and he was recommended to an auld limmer – Janet M'Clour, they ca'ed her – and sae far left to himsel' as to be ower persuaded. There was mony advised him to the contrar, for Janet was mair than suspeckit by the best folk in Ba'weary. Lang or that, she had had a wean to a dragoon; she hadnae come forrit [2] for maybe thretty year; and bairns had seen her mumblin' to hersel' up on Key's Loan in the gloamin', whilk was an unco time an' place for a God-fearin' woman. Howsoever, it was the laird himsel' that had first tauld the minister o' Janet; and in thae days he wad have gane a far gate to pleesure the laird. When folk tauld him that Janet was sib to the deil, it was a' superstition by his way of it; an' when they cast up the Bible to him an' the witch of Endor, he wad threep it doun their thrapples that thir days were a' gane by, and the deil was mercifully restrained.

Weel, when it got about the clachan that Janet M'Clour was to be servant at the manse, the folk were fair mad wi' her an' him thegether; and some o' the guidwives had nae better to dae than get round her door cheeks and chairge her wi' a' that was ken't again her, frae the sodger's bairn to John Tamson's twa kye. She was nae great speaker; folk usually let her gang her ain gate, an' she let them gang theirs, wi' neither Fair-gui-deen nor Fair-guid-day; but when she buckled to, she had a tongue to deave the miller. Up she got, an' there wasnae an auld story in Ba'weary but she gart somebody lowp for it that day; they couldnae say ae thing but she could say twa to it; till, at the hinder end, the guidwives up and claught hand of her, and clawed the coats aff her back, and pu'd her doun the clachan to the water o' Dule, to see if she were a witch or no, soum or droun. The carline skirled till ye could hear her at the Hangin' Shaw, and she focht like ten; there was mony a guidwife bure the mark of her neist day an' mony a lang day after; and just in the hettest o' the collieshangie, wha suld come up (for his sins) but the new minister.

"Women," said he (and he had a grand voice), "I

charge you in the Lord's name to let her go."

Janet ran to him — she was fair wud wi' terror — an' clang to him, an' prayed him, for Christ's sake, save her frae the cummers; an' they, for their part, tauld him a' that was ken't, and maybe mair.

"Woman," says he to Janet, "is this true?"

"As the Lord sees me," says she, "as the Lord made me, no a word o't. Forbye the bairn," says she, "I've been a decent woman a' my days."

"Will you," says Mr. Soulis, "in the name of God, and before me, His unworthy minister, renounce the devil and his works?"

Weel, it wad appear that when he askit that, she gave a girn that fairly frichtit them that saw her, an' they could hear her teeth play dirl thegether in her chafts; but there was naething for it but the ae way or the ither; an' Janet lifted up her hand and renounced the deil before them a'.

"And now," says Mr. Soulis to the guidwives, "home with ye, one and all, and pray to God for His forgiveness."

And he gied Janet his arm, though she had little on her but a sark, and took her up the clachan to her ain door like a leddy of the land; an' her scrieghin, and laughin' as was a scandal to be heard.

There were mony grave folk lang ower their prayers that nicht; but when the morn cam' there was sic a fear fell upon a' Ba'weary that the bairns hid theirsels, and even the men folk stood and keekit frae their doors. For there was Janet comin' doun the clachan — her or her likeness, nane could tell — wi' her neck thrawn, and her held on ae side, like a body that has been hangit, and a grin on her face like an unstreakit corp. By an' by they got used wi' it, and even speered at her to ken what was wrang; but frae that day forth she couldnae speak like a Christian woman, but slavered and played click wi' her teeth like a pair o' shears; and frae that day forth the name o' God cam' never on her lips. Whiles she wad try to say it, but it michtnae be. Them that kenned best said least; but they never gied that Thing the name o' Janet M'Clour; for the auld Janet, by their way o't, was in muckle hell that day. But the minister was neither to haud nor to bind; he preached about naething but the folk's cruelty that had gi'en her a stroke of the palsy; he skelpt the bairns that meddled her; and he had her up to the manse that same nicht, and dwalled there a' his lane wi' her under the Hangin' Shaw.

Weel, time gaed by: and the idler sort commenced to think mair lichtly o' that black business. The minister was weel thocht o'; he was aye late at the writing, folk wad see his can'le doon by the Dule water after twal' at e'en; and he seemed pleased wi' himsel' and upsitten as at first, though a' body could see that he was dwining. As for Janet she cam' an' she gaed; if she didnae speak muckle afore, it was reason she should speak less then; she meddled naebody; but she was an eldritch thing to see, an' nane wad hae mistrysted wi' her for Ba'weary glebe.

About the end o' July there cam' a spell o' weather, the like o't never was in that countryside; it was lown an' het an' heartless; the herds couldnae win up the Black Hill, the bairns were ower weariet to play; an' yet it was gousty too, wi' claps o' het wund that rummled in the glens, and bits o' shouers that slockened naething. We aye thocht it but to thun'er on the morn; but the morn cam', an' the morn's morning, and it was aye the same uncanny weather, sair on folks and bestial. Of a' that were the waur, nane suffered like Mr. Soulis; he could neither sleep nor eat, he tauld his elders; an' when he wasnae writin' at his weary book, he wad be stravaguin' ower a' the countryside like a man possessed, when a' body else was blythe to keep caller ben the house.

Abune Hangin' Shaw, in the bield o' the Black Hill, there's a bit enclosed grund wi' an iron yett; and it seems, in the auld days, that was the kirkyaird o' Ba'weary, and consecrated by the Papists before the blessed licht shone upon the kingdom. It was a great howff, o' Mr. Soulis's onyway; there he would sit an' consider his sermons; and inded it's a bieldy bit. Weel, as he cam' ower the wast end o' the Black Hill, ae day, he saw first twa, an' syne fower, an' syne seeven corbie craws fleein' round an' round abune the auld kirkyaird. They flew laigh and heavy, an' squawked to ither as they gaed; and it was clear to Mr. Soulis that something had put them frae their ordinar. He wasnae easy fleyed, an' gaed straucht up to the wa's; and what suld he find there but a man, or the appearance of a man, sittin' in the inside upon a grave. He was of a great stature, an' black as hell, and his e'en were singular to see. [3] Mr. Soulis had heard tell o' black men mony's the time; but there was something unco about this black man that daunted him. Het as he was, he took a kind o' cauld grue in the marrow o' his banes; but up he spak for a' that; an' says he: "My friend, are you a stranger in this place?" The black man answered never a word; he got upon his feet, an' begude to hirsle to the wa' on the far side; but he aye lookit at the minister; an' the minister stood an' lookit back; till a' in a meenute the black man was ower the wa' an' runnin' for the bield o' the trees. Mr. Soulis, he hardly kenned why, ran after him; but he was sair forjaskit wi' his walk an' the het, unhalsome weather; and rin as he likit, he got nae mair than a glisk o' the black man amang the birks, till he won doun to the foot o' the hillside, an' there he saw him ance mair, gaun, hap, step, an' lowp, ower Dule water to the manse.

Mr. Soulis wasnae weel pleased that this fearsome gangrel suld mak' sae free wi' Ba'weary manse; an' he ran the harder, an' wet shoon, ower the burn, an' up the walk; but the deil a black man was there to see. He stepped out upon the road, but there was naebody there; he gaed a' ower the gairden, but na, nae black man. At the binder end, and a bit feared as was but natural, he lifted the hasp and into the manse; and there was Janet M'Clour before his een, wi' her thrawn craig, and nane sae pleased to see him. And he aye minded sinsyne, when first he set his een upon her, he had the same cauld and deidly grue.

"Janet," says he, "have you seen a black man?"

"A black man!" quo' she. "Save us a'! Ye're no wise, minister. There's nae black man in a' Ba'weary."

But she didnae speak plain, ye maun understand; but yam-yammered, like a powny wi' the bit in its moo.

"Weel," says he, "Janet, if there was nae black man, I have spoken with the Accuser of the Brethren."

And he sat doun like ane wi' a fever, an' his teeth chittered in his heid.

"Hoots," says she, "think shame to yoursel', minister"; and gied him a drap brandy that she keept aye by her.

Syne Mr. Soulis gaed into his study amang a' his

books. It's a lang, laigh, mirk chalmer, perishin' cauld in winter, an' no very dry even in the top o' the simmer, for the manse stands near the burn. Sae doun he sat, and thocht of a' that had come an' gane since he was in Ba'weary, an' his hame, an' the days when he was a bairn an' ran daffin' on the braes; and that black man aye ran in his held like the owercome of a sang. Aye the mair he thocht, the mair he thocht o' the black man. He tried the prayer, an' the words wouldnae come to him; an' he tried, they say, to write at his book, but he couldnae mak' nae mair o' that. There was whiles he thocht the black man was at his oxter, an' the swat stood upon him cauld as well-water; and there was other whiles, when he cam' to himsel' like a christened bairn and minded naething.

The upshot was that he gaed to the window an' stood glowrin' at Dule water. The trees are unco thick, an' the water lies deep an' black under the manse; and there was Janet washin' the cla'es wi' her coats kilted. She had her back to the minister, an' he, for his pairt, hardly kenned what he was lookin' at. Syne she turned round, an' shawed her face: Mr. Soulis had the same cauld grue as twice that day afore, an' it was borne in upon him what folk said, that Janet was deid lang syne, an' this was a bogle in her clay-cauld flesh. He drew back a pickle and he scanned her narrowly. She was tramp-trampin' in the cla'es, croonin' to hersel'; and eh! Gude guide us, but it was a fearsome face. Whiles she sang louder, but there was nae man born o' woman that could tell the words o' her sang; an' whiles she lookit side-lang doun, but there was naething there for her to look at. There gaed a scunner through the flesh upon his banes; and that was Heeven's advertisement. But Mr. Soulis just blamed himsel', he said, to think sae ill of a puir, auld afflicted wife that hadnae a freend forbye himsel'; an' he put up a bit prayer for him an' her, an' drank a little caller water — for his heart rose again the meat — an' gaed up to his naked bed in the gloaming.

That was a nicht that has never been forgotten in Ba'weary, the nicht o' the seeventeenth of August, seventeen hun'er' an' twal'. It had been het afore, as I hae said, but that nicht it was better than ever. The sun gaed doun amang unco-lookin' clouds; it fell as mirk as the pit; no a star, no a breath o' wund; ye couldnae see your han' afore your face, and even the auld folk cuist the covers frae their beds and lay pechin' for their breath. Wi' a' that he had upon his mind, it was gey and unlikely Mr. Soulis wad get muckle sleep. He lay an' he tummled; the gude, caller bed that he got into brunt his very banes; whiles he slept, and whiles he waukened; whiles he heard the time o' nicht, and whiles a tyke yowlin' up the muir, as if somebody was deid; whiles he thocht he heard bogles claverin' in his lug, an' whiles he saw spunkies in the room. He behoved, he judged, to be sick; an' sick he was — little he jaloosed the sickness.

At the hinder end, he got a clearness in his mind, sat up in his sark on the bed-side, and fell thinkin' ance mair o' the black man an' Janet. He couldnae weel tell how — maybe it was the cauld to his feet — but it cam' in up upon him wi' a spate that there was some connection between thir twa, an' that either or baith o' them were bogles. And just at that moment, in Janet's room, which was neist to his, there cam' a stramp o' feet as if men were wars'lin', an' then a loud bang; an' then a wund gaed reishling round the fower quarters of the house; an' then a' was ance mair as seelent as the grave.

Mr. Soulis was feared for neither man nor deevil. He got his tinder-box, an' lit a can'le. He made three steps o't ower to Janet's door. It was on the hasp, an' he pushed it open, an' keeked bauldly in. It was a big room, as big as the minister's ain, a' plenished wi' grand, auld, solid gear, for he had nathing else. There was a fower-posted bed wi' auld tapestry; and a braw cabinet of aik, that was fu' o' the minister's divinity books, an' put there to be out o' the gate; an' a wheen duds o' Janet's lying here and there about the floor. But nae Janet could Mr. Soulis see; nor ony sign of a contention. In he gaed (an' there's few that wad ha'e followed him) an' lookit a' round, an' listened. But there was naethin' to be heard, neither inside the manse nor in a' Ba'weary parish, an' naethin' to be seen but the muckle shadows turnin' round the can'le. An' then, a' at ance, the minister's heart played dunt an' stood stock-still; an' a cauld wund blew amang the hairs o' his heid. Whaten a weary sicht was that for the puir man's een! For there was Janet hangin' frae a nail beside the auld aik cabinet: her heid aye lay on her shouther, her een were steeked, the tongue projeckit frae her mouth, and her heels were twa feet clear abune the floor.

"God forgive us all!" thocht Mr. Soulis, "poor Janet's dead."

He cam' a step nearer to the corp; an' then his heart fair whammled in his inside. For by what cantrip it wad ill-beseem a man to judge, she was hingin' frae a single nail an' by a single wursted thread for darnin' hose.

It's a awfu' thing to be your lane at nicht wi' siccan prodigies o' darkness; but Mr. Soulis was strong in the Lord. He turned an' gaed his ways oot o' that room, and lockit the door ahint him; and step by step, doon the stairs, as heavy as leed; and set doon the can'le on the table at the stairfoot. He couldnae pray, he couldnae think, he was dreepin' wi' caul' swat, an' naething could he hear but the dunt-dunt-duntin' o' his ain heart. He micht maybe have stood there an hour, or maybe twa, he minded sae little; when a' o' a sudden, he heard a laigh, uncanny steer up-stairs; a foot gaed to an' fro in the chalmer whaur the corp was hingin'; syne the door was opened, though he minded weel that he had lockit it; an' syne there was a step upon the landin', an' it seemed to him as if the corp was lookin' ower the rail and doun upon him whaur he stood.

He took up the can'le again (for he couldnae want the licht), and as saftly as ever he could, gaed straucht out o' the manse an' to the far end o' the causeway. It was aye pit-mirk; the flame o' th can'le, when he set it on the grund, brunt steedy an clear as in a room; naething moved, but the Dule water seepin' and sabbin' doon the glen, an' yon unhaly footstep that cam' ploddin' doun the stairs inside the manse. He kenned the foot ower weel, for it was Janet's; and at ilka step that cam' a wee thing nearer, the cauld got deeper in his vitals. He commended his soul to Him that made an' keepit him; "and O Lord," said he, "give me strength this night to war against the powers of evil."

By this time the foot was comin' through the passage for the door; he could hear a hand skirt alang the wa', as if the fearsome thing was feelin' for its way. The saughs tossed an' maned thegether, a long sigh cam' ower the hills, the flame o' the can'le was blawn aboot; an' there stood the corp of Thrawn Janet, wi' her grogram goun an' her black mutch, wi' the heid upon the shouther, an' the grin still upon the face o't — leevin', ye wad he said — deid, as Mr. Soulis weel kenned — upon the threshold o' the manse.

It's a strange thing that the saul of man should be that thirled into his perishable body; but the minister saw that, an' his heart didnae break.

She didnae stand there lang; she began to move again an' cam' slowly towards Mr. Soulis whaur he stood under the saughs. A' the life o' his body, a' the strength o' his speerit, were glowerin' frae his een. It seemed she was gaun to speak, but wanted words, an' made a sign wi' the left hand. There cam' a clap o' wund, like a cat's fuff; oot gaed the can'le, the saughs skrieghed like folk; an' Mr. Soulis keened that, live or die, this was the end o't.

"Witch, beldame, devil!" he cried, "I charge you, by the power of God, begone — if you be dead, to the grave — if you be damned, to hell."

An' at that moment the Lord's ain hand out o' the Heevens struck the Horror whaur it stood; the auld, deid, desecrated corp o' the witch-wife, sae lang keepit frae the grave and hirsled round by deils, lowed up like a brunstane spunk and fell in ashes to the grund; the thunder followed, peal on dirling peal, the rairing rain upon the back o' that; and Mr. Soulis lowped through the garden hedge, and ran, wi' skelloch upon skelloch, for the clachan.

That same mornin', John Christie saw the Black Man pass the Muckle Cairn as it was chappin' six; before eicht, he gaed by the change-house at Knockdow; an' no lang after, Sandy M'Lellan saw him gaun linkin' doun the braes frae Kilmackerlie. There's little doubt but it was him that dwalled se lang in Janet's body; but he was awa' at last; and sinsyne the deil has never fashed us in Ba'weary.

But it was a sair dispensation for the minister; lang, lang he lay ravin' in his bed; and frae that hour to this, he was the man ye ken the day.

*****

[2] To come forrit – to offer oneself as a communicant.

[3] It was a common belief in Scotland that the devil appeared as a black man. This appears in several witch trials and I think in Law's *Memorials,* that delightful storehouse of the quaint and grisly.

VIII. The Yellow Cat – Wilbur Daniel Steele

At least once in my life I have had the good fortune to board a deserted vessel at sea. I say "good fortune" because it has left me the memory of a singular impression. I have felt a ghost of the same thing two or three times since then, when peeping through the doorway of an abandoned house.

Now that vessel was not dead. She was a good vessel, a sound vessel, even a handsome vessel, in her blunt-bowed, coastwise way. She sailed under four lowers across as blue and glittering a sea as I have ever known, and there was not a point in her sailing that one could lay a finger upon as wrong. And yet, passing that schooner at two miles, one knew, somehow, that no hand was on her wheel. Sometimes I can imagine a vessel, stricken like that, moving over the empty spaces of the sea, carrying it off quite well were it not for that indefinable suggestion of a stagger; and I can think of all those ocean gods, in whom no landsman will ever believe, looking at one another and tapping their foreheads with just the shadow of a smile.

I wonder if they all scream – these ships that have lost their souls? Mine screamed. We heard her voice, like nothing I have ever heard before, when we rowed under her counter to read her name – the *Marionnette* it was, of Halifax. I remember how it made me shiver, there in the full blaze of the sun, to hear her going on so, railing and screaming in that stark fashion. And I remember, too, how our footsteps, pattering through the vacant internals in search of that haggard utterance, made me think of the footsteps of hurrying warders roused in the night.

And we found a parrot in a cage; that was all. It

wanted water. We gave it water and went away to look things over, keeping pretty close together, all of us. In the quarters the table was set for four. Two men had begun to eat, by the evidences of the plates. Nowhere in the vessel was there any sign of disorder, except one sea-chest broken out, evidently in haste. Her papers were gone and the stern davits were empty. That is how the case stood that day, and that is how it has stood to this. I saw this same *Marionnette* a week later, tied up to a Hoboken dock, where she awaited news from her owners; but even there, in the midst of all the water-front bustle, I could not get rid of the feeling that she was still very far away — in a sort of shippish other-world.

The thing happens now and then. Sometimes half a dozen years will go by without a solitary wanderer of this sort crossing the ocean paths, and then in a single season perhaps several of them will turn up: vacant waifs, impassive and mysterious — a quarter-column of tidings tucked away on the second page of the evening paper.

That is where I read the story about the *Abbie Rose*. I recollect how painfully awkward and out-of-place it looked there, cramped between ruled black edges and smelling of landsman's ink — this thing that had to do essentially with air and vast coloured spaces. I forget the exact words of the heading — something like "Abandoned Craft Picked Up At Sea" — but I still have the clipping itself, couched in the formal patter of the marine-news writer:

The first hint of another mystery of the sea came in to-day when the schooner *Abbie Rose* dropped anchor in the upper river, manned only by a crew of one. It appears that the outbound freighter *Mercury* sighted the *Abbie Rose* off Block Island on Thursday last, acting in a suspicious manner. A boat-party sent aboard found the schooner in perfect order and condition, sailing under four lower sails, the topsails being pursed up to the mastheads but not stowed. With the exception of a yellow cat, the vessel was found to be utterly deserted, though her small boat still hung in the davits. No evidences of disorder were visible in any part of the craft. The dishes were washed up, the stove in the galley was still slightly warm to the touch, everything in its proper place with the exception of the vessel's papers, which were not to be found.

All indications being for fair weather, Captain Rohmer of the *Mercury* detailed two of his company to bring the find back to this port, a distance of one hundred and fifteen miles. The only man available with a knowledge of the fore-and-aft rig was Stewart McCord, the second engineer. A seaman by the name of Björnsen was sent with him. McCord arrived this noon, after a very heavy voyage of five days, reporting that Björnsen had fallen overboard while shaking out the foretopsail. McCord himself showed evidence of the hardships he has passed through, being almost a nervous wreck.

Stewart McCord! Yes, Stewart McCord would have a knowledge of the fore-and-aft rig, or of almost anything else connected with the affairs of the sea. It happened that I used to know this fellow. I had even been quite chummy with him in the old days — that is, to the extent of drinking too many beers with him in certain hot-country ports. I remembered him as a stolid and deliberate sort of a person, with an amazing hodgepodge of learning, a stamp collection, and a theory about the effects of tropical sunshine on the Caucasian race, to which I have listened half of more than one night, stretched out naked on a freighter's deck. He had not impressed me as a fellow who would be bothered by his nerves.

And there was another thing about the story which struck me as rather queer. Perhaps it is a relic of my seafaring days, but I have always been a conscientious reader of the weather reports; and I could remember no weather in the past week sufficient to shake a man out of a top, especially a man by the name of Björnsen — a thoroughgoing seafaring name.

I was destined to hear more of this in the evening, from the ancient boatman who rowed me out on the upper river. He had been to sea in his day. He knew enough to wonder about this thing, even to indulge in a little superstitious awe about it.

"No sir-ee. Something *happened* to them four chaps. And another thing — "

I fancied I heard a sea-bird whining in the darkness overhead. A shape moved out of the gloom ahead, passed to the left, lofty and silent, and merged once more with the gloom behind — a barge at anchor, with the sea-grass clinging around her waterline.

"Funny about that other chap," the old fellow speculated. "Björnsen — I b'lieve he called 'im. Now that story sounds to me kind of — " He feathered his oars with a suspicious jerk and peered at me. "This McCord a friend of yourn?" he inquired.

"In a way," I said.

"Hm-m — well — " He turned on his thwart to squint ahead. "There she is," he announced, with something of relief, I thought.

It was hard at that time of night to make anything but a black blotch out of the *Abbie Rose*. Of course I could see that she was pot-bellied, like the rest of the coastwise sisterhood. And that McCord had not stowed his topsails. I could make them out, pursed at the mastheads and hanging down as far as the cross-trees, like huge, over-ripe pears. Then I recollected that he had found them so – probably had not touched them since; a queer way to leave tops, it seemed to me. I could see also the glowing tip of a cigar floating restlessly along the farther rail. I called: "McCord! Oh, McCord!"

The spark came swimming across the deck. "Hello! Hello, there – ah – " There was a note of querulous uneasiness there that somehow jarred with my remembrance of this man.

"Ridgeway," I explained.

He echoed the name uncertainly, still with that suggestion of peevishness, hanging over the rail and peering down at us. "Oh! By gracious!" he exclaimed, abruptly. "I'm glad to see you, Ridgeway. I had a boatman coming out before this, but I guess – well, I guess he'll be along. By gracious! I'm glad – "

"I'll not keep you," I told the gnome, putting the money in his palm and reaching for the rail. McCord lent me a hand on my wrist. Then when I stood squarely on the deck beside him he appeared to forget my presence, leaned forward heavily on the rail, and squinted after my waning boatman.

"Ahoy – boat!" he called out, sharply, shielding his lips with his hand. His violence seemed to bring him out of the blank, for he fell immediately to puffing strongly at his cigar and explaining in rather a shame-voiced way that he was beginning to think his own boatman had "passed him up."

"Come in and have a nip," he urged with an abrupt heartiness, clapping me on the shoulder.

"So you've — " I did not say what I had intended. I was thinking that in the old days McCord had made rather a fetish of touching nothing stronger than beer. Neither had he been of the shoulder-clapping sort. "So you've got something aboard?" I shifted.

"Dead men's liquor," he chuckled. It gave me a queer feeling in the pit of my stomach to hear him. I began to wish I had not come, but there was nothing for it now but to follow him into the after-house. The cabin itself might have been nine feet square, with three bunks occupying the port side. To the right opened the master's stateroom, and a door in the forward bulkhead led to the galley.

I took in these features at a casual glance. Then, hardly knowing why I did it, I began to examine them with greater care.

"Have you a match?" I asked. My voice sounded very small, as though something unheard of had happened to all the air.

"Smoke?" he asked. "I'll get you a cigar."

"No." I took the proffered match, scratched it on the side of the galley door, and passed out. There seemed to be a thousand pans there, throwing my match back at me from every wall of the box-like compartment. Even McCord's eyes, in the doorway, were large and round and shining. He probably thought me crazy. Perhaps I was, a little. I ran the match along close to the ceiling and came upon a rusty hook a little aport of the centre.

"There," I said. "Was there anything hanging from this — er — say a parrot — or something,

McCord?" The match burned my fingers and went out.

"What do you mean?" McCord demanded from the doorway. I got myself back into the comfortable yellow glow of the cabin before I answered, and then it was a question.

"Do you happen to know anything about this craft's personal history?"

"No. What are you talking about! Why?"

"Well, I do," I offered. "For one thing, she's changed her name. And it happens this isn't the first time she's — Well, damn it all, fourteen years ago I helped pick up this whatever-she-is off the Virginia Capes — in the same sort of condition. There you are!" I was yapping like a nerve-strung puppy.

McCord leaned forward with his hands on the table, bringing his face beneath the fan of the hanging-lamp. For the first time I could mark how shockingly it had changed. It was almost colourless. The jaw had somehow lost its old-time security and the eyes seemed to be loose in their sockets. I had expected him to start at my announcement; he only blinked at the light.

"I am not surprised," he remarked at length. "After what I've seen and heard — " He lifted his fist and brought it down with a sudden crash on the table. "Man — let's have a nip!"

He was off before I could say a word, fumbling out of sight in the narrow stateroom. Presently he reappeared, holding a glass in either hand and a dark bottle hugged between his elbows. Putting the glasses down, he held up the bottle between his eyes and the lamp, and its shadow, falling across his face, green and luminous at the core, gave him a ghastly look — like a mutilation or an unspeakable birthmark. He shook the bottle gently and chuckled his "Dead men's liquor" again. Then he poured two half-glasses of the clear gin, swallowed his portion, and sat down.

"A parrot," he mused, a little of the liquor's colour creeping into his cheeks. "No, this time it was a cat, Ridgeway. A yellow cat. She was — "

"*Was?*" I caught him up. "What's happened — what's become of her?"

"Vanished. Evaporated. I haven't seen her since night before last, when I caught her trying to lower the boat — "

"*Stop it!*" It was I who banged the table now, without any of the reserve of decency. "McCord, you're drunk — *drunk*, I tell you. A *cat*! Let a *cat* throw you off your head like this! She's probably hiding out below this minute, on affairs of her own."

"Hiding?" He regarded me for a moment with the queer superiority of the damned. "I guess you don't realize how many times I've been over this hulk, from decks to keelson, with a mallet and a foot-rule."

"Or fallen overboard," I shifted, with less assurance. "Like this fellow Björnsen. By the way, McCord — " I stopped there on account of the look in his eyes.

He reached out, poured himself a shot, swallowed it, and got up to shuffle about the confined quarters. I watched their restless circuit — my friend and his jumping shadow. He stopped and bent forward to examine a Sunday-supplement chromo tacked on the wall, and the two heads drew together, as though there were something to whisper. Of a sudden I seemed to hear the old gnome croaking, "Now that story sounds to me kind of — "

McCord straightened up and turned to face me.

"What do you know about Björnsen?" he demanded.

"Well — only what they had you saying in the papers," I told him.

"Pshaw!" He snapped his fingers, tossing the affair aside. "I found her log," he announced in quite another voice.

"You did, eh? I judged, from what I read in the paper, that there wasn't a sign."

"No, no; I happened on this the other night, under the mattress in there." He jerked his head toward the stateroom. "Wait!" I heard him knocking things over in the dark and mumbling at them. After a moment he came out and threw on the table a long, cloth-covered ledger, of the common commercial sort. It lay open at about the middle, showing close script running indiscriminately across the column ruling.

"When I said 'log,'" he went on, "I guess I was going it a little strong. At least, I wouldn't want that sort of log found around *my* vessel. Let's call it a personal record. Here's his picture, somewhere — " He shook the book by its back and a common kodak blue-print fluttered to the table. It was the likeness of a solid man with a paunch, a huge square beard, small squinting eyes, and a bald head. "What do you make of him — a writing chap?"

"From the nose down, yes," I estimated. "From the nose up, he will 'tend to his own business if you will 'tend to yours, strictly."

McCord slapped his thigh. "By gracious! that's

the fellow! He hates the Chinaman. He knows as well as anything he ought not to put down in black and white how intolerably he hates the Chinaman, and yet he must sneak off to his cubby-hole and suck his pencil, and — how is it Stevenson has it? — the 'agony of composition,' you remember. Can you imagine the fellow, Ridgeway, bundling down here with the fever on him — "

"About the Chinaman," I broke in. "I think you said something about a Chinaman?"

"Yes. The cook, he must have been. I gather he wasn't the master's pick, by the reading-matter here. Probably clapped on to him by the owners — shifted from one of their others at the last moment; a queer trick. Listen." He picked up the book and, running over the pages with a selective thumb, read:

"*August second.* — First part, moderate southwesterly breeze —

and so forth — er — but here he comes to it:

"Anything can happen to a man at sea, even a funeral. In special to a Chinyman, who is of no account to social welfare, being a barbarian as I look at it.

"Something of a philosopher, you see. And did you get the reserve in that 'even a funeral'? An artist, I tell you. But wait: let me catch him a bit wilder. Here:

"I'll get that mustard-coloured — — [This is back a couple of days.] Never can hear the — — coming, in them carpet slippers. Turned round and found him standing right to my back this morning. Could have stuck a knife into me easy. 'Look here!' says I, and fetched him a tap on the ear that will make him walk louder next time, I warrant. He could have stuck a knife into me easy.

"A clear case of moral funk, I should say. Can you imagine the fellow, Ridgeway — "

"Yes; oh, yes." I was ready with a phrase of my own. "A man handicapped with an imagination. You see he can't quite understand this 'barbarian,' who has him beaten by about thirty centuries of civilization — and his imagination has to have something to chew on, something to hit — a 'tap on the ear,' you know."

"By gracious! that's the ticket!" McCord pounded his knee. "And now we've got another chap going to pieces — Peters, he calls him. Refuses to eat dinner on August the third, claiming he caught the Chink making passes over the chowder-pot with his thumb. Can you believe it, Ridgeway — in this very cabin here?" Then he went on with a suggestion of haste, as though he had somehow made a slip. "Well, at any rate, the disease seems to be catching. Next day it's Bach, the second seaman, who begins to feel the gaff. Listen:

"Bach he comes to me to-night, complaining he's being watched. He claims the — — has got the evil eye. Says he can see you through a two-inch bulkhead, and the like. The Chink's laying in his bunk, turned the other way. 'Why don't you go aboard of him?' says I. The Dutcher says nothing, but goes over to his own bunk and feels under the straw. When he comes back he's looking queer. 'By God!' says he, 'the devil has swiped my gun!' ... Now if that's true there is going to be hell to pay in this vessel very quick. I figure I'm still master of this vessel."

"The evil eye," I grunted. "Consciences gone wrong there somewhere."

"Not altogether, Ridgeway. I can see that yellow man peeking. Now just figure yourself, say, eight thousand miles from home, out on the water alone with a crowd of heathen fanatics crazy from fright, looking around for guns and so on. Don't you believe you'd keep an eye around the corners, kind of — eh? I'll bet a hat he was taking it all in, lying there in his bunk, 'turned the other way.' Eh? I pity the poor cuss — Well, there's only one more entry after that. He's good and mad. Here:

"Now, by God! this is the end. My gun's gone, too; right out from under lock and key, by God! I been talking with Bach this morning. Not to let on, I had him in to clean my lamp. There's more ways than one, he says, and so do I."

McCord closed the book and dropped it on the table. "Finis," he said. "The rest is blank paper."

"Well!" I will confess I felt much better than I had for some time past. "There's *one* 'mystery of the sea' gone to pot, at any rate. And now, if you don't mind, I think I'll have another of your nips, McCord."

He pushed my glass across the table and got up, and behind his back his shadow rose to scour the corners of the room, like an incorruptible sentinel. I forgot to take up my gin, watching him. After an uneasy minute or so he came back to the table and pressed the tip of a forefinger on the book.

"Ridgeway," he said, "you don't seem to understand. This particular 'mystery of the sea' hasn't been scratched yet — not even *scratched*, Ridgeway." He sat down and leaned forward, fixing me with a didactic finger. "What happened?"

"Well, I have an idea the 'barbarian' got them, when it came to the pinch."

"And let the — remains over the side?"

"I should say."

"And they came back and got the 'barbarian' and let *him* over the side, eh? There were none left, you remember."

"Oh, good Lord, I don't know!" I flared with a childish resentment at this catechizing of his. But his finger remained there, challenging.

"I do," he announced. "The Chinaman put them over the side, as we have said. And then, after that, he died — of wounds about the head."

"So?" I had still sarcasm.

"You will remember," he went on, "that the skipper did not happen to mention a cat, a *yellow* cat, in his confessions."

"McCord," I begged him, "please drop it. Why in thunder *should* he mention a cat?"

"True. Why *should* he mention a cat? I think one of the reasons why he should *not* mention a cat is because there did not happen to be a cat aboard at that time."

"Oh, all right!" I reached out and pulled the bottle to my side of the table. Then I took out my watch. "If you don't mind," I suggested, "I think we'd better be going ashore. I've got to get to my office rather early in the morning. What do you say?"

He said nothing for the moment, but his finger had dropped. He leaned back and stared straight into the core of the light above, his eyes squinting.

"He would have been from the south of China, probably." He seemed to be talking to himself. "There's a considerable sprinkling of the belief down there, I've heard. It's an uncanny business — this transmigration of souls — "

Personally, I had had enough of it. McCord's fingers came groping across the table for the bottle. I picked it up hastily and let it go through the open companionway, where it died with a faint gurgle, out somewhere on the river.

"Now," I said to him, shaking the vagrant wrist, "either you come ashore with me or you go in there and get under the blankets. You're drunk, McCord — *drunk*. Do you hear me?"

"Ridgeway," he pronounced, bringing his eyes down to me and speaking very slowly. "You're a fool, if you can't see better than that. I'm not drunk. I'm sick. I haven't slept for three nights — and now I can't. And you say — you — " He went to pieces very suddenly, jumped up, pounded the legs of his chair on the decking, and shouted at me: "And you say that, you — you landlubber, you office coddler! You're so comfortably sure that everything in the world is cut and dried. Come back to the water again and learn how to wonder — and stop talking like a damn fool. Do you know where — Is there anything in your municipal budget to tell me where Björnsen went? Listen!" He sat down, waving me to do the same, and went on with a sort of desperate repression.

"It happened on the first night after we took this hellion. I'd stood the wheel most of the afternoon — off and on, that is, because she sails herself uncommonly well. Just put her on a reach, you know, and she carries it off pretty well — "

"I know," I nodded.

"Well, we mugged up about seven o'clock. There

was a good deal of canned stuff in the galley, and Björnsen wasn't a bad hand with a kettle — a thoroughgoing Square-head he was — tall and lean and yellow-haired, with little fat, round cheeks and a white moustache. Not a bad chap at all. He took the wheel to stand till midnight, and I turned in, but I didn't drop off for quite a spell. I could hear his boots wandering around over my head, padding off forward, coming back again. I heard him whistling now and then — an outlandish air. Occasionally I could see the shadow of his head waving in a block of moonlight that lay on the decking right down there in front of the stateroom door. It came from the companion; the cabin was dark because we were going easy on the oil. They hadn't left a great deal, for some reason or other."

McCord leaned back and described with his finger where the illumination had cut the decking.

"There! I could see it from my bunk, as I lay, you understand. I must have almost dropped off once when I heard him fiddling around out here in the cabin, and then he said something in a whisper, just to find out if I was still awake, I suppose. I asked him what the matter was. He came and poked his head in the door."

"'The breeze is going out,' says he. 'I was wondering if we couldn't get a little more sail on her.' Only I can't give you his fierce Square-head tang. 'How about the tops?' he suggested.

"I was so sleepy I didn't care, and I told him so. 'All right,' he says, 'but I thought I might shake out one of them tops.' Then I heard him blow at something outside. 'Scat, you — — !' Then: 'This cat's going to set me crazy, Mr. McCord,' he says, 'following me around everywhere.' He gave a kick, and I saw something yellow floating across the moonlight. It never made a sound — just floated. You wouldn't have known it ever lit anywhere, just like — "

McCord stopped and drummed a few beats on the table with his fist, as though to bring himself back to the straight narrative.

"I went to sleep," he began again. "I dreamed about a lot of things. I woke up sweating. You know how glad you are to wake up after a dream like that and find none of it is so? Well, I turned over and settled to go off again, and then I got a little more awake and thought to myself it must be pretty near time for me to go on deck. I scratched a match and looked at my watch. 'That fellow must be either a good chap or asleep,' I said to myself. And I rolled out quick and went above-decks. He wasn't at the wheel. I called him: 'Björnsen! Björnsen!' No answer."

McCord was really telling a story now. He paused for a long moment, one hand shielding an ear and his eyeballs turned far up.

"That was the first time I really went over the hulk," he ran on. "I got out a lantern and started at the forward end of the hold, and I worked aft, and there was nothing there. Not a sign, or a stain, or a scrap of clothing, or anything. You may believe that I began to feel funny inside. I went over the decks and the rails and the house itself — inch by inch. Not a trace. I went out aft again. The cat sat on the wheel-box, washing her face. I hadn't noticed the scar on her head before, running down between her ears — rather a new scar — three or four days old, I should say. It looked ghastly and blue-white in the flat moonlight. I ran over and grabbed her up to heave her over the side — you understand how upset I was. Now you know a cat will squirm around and grab something when you hold it like that, generally speaking. This one didn't. She just drooped and began to purr and looked up at me out of her moonlit eyes under that scar. I dropped her on the deck and backed off. You remember Björnsen had *kicked* her — and I didn't want anything like that happening to — "

The narrator turned upon me with a sudden heat, leaned over and shook his finger before my face.

"There you go!" he cried. "You, with your stout stone buildings and your policemen and your neighbourhood church — you're so damn sure. But I'd just like to see you out there, alone, with the moon setting, and all the lights gone tall and queer, and a shipmate — " He lifted his hand overhead, the finger-tips pressed together and then suddenly separated as though he had released an impalpable something into the air.

"Go on," I told him.

"I felt more like you do, when it got light again, and warm and sunshiny. I said 'Bah!' to the whole business. I even fed the cat, and I slept awhile on the roof of the house — I was so sure. We lay dead most of the day, without a streak of air. But that night — ! Well, that night I hadn't got over being sure yet. It takes quite a jolt, you know, to shake loose several dozen generations. A fair, steady breeze had come along, the glass was high, she was staying herself like a doll, and so I figured I could get a little rest, lying below in the bunk, even if I didn't sleep.

"I tried not to sleep, in case something should come up — a squall or the like. But I think I must have dropped off once or twice. I remember I heard something fiddling around in the galley, and I hollered 'Scat!' and everything was quiet again. I rolled over and lay on my left side, staring at that square of moonlight outside my door for a long time. You'll think it was a dream — what I saw there."

"Go on," I said.

"Call this table-top the spot of light, roughly," he said. He placed a finger-tip at about the middle of the forward edge and drew it slowly toward the centre. "Here, what would correspond with the upper side of the companionway, there came down very gradually the shadow of a tail. I watched it streaking out there across the deck, wiggling the slightest bit now and then. When it had come down about half-way across the light, the solid part of the animal — its shadow, you understand — began to appear, quite big and round. But how could she hang there, done up in a ball, from the hatch?"

He shifted his finger back to the edge of the table and puddled it around to signify the shadowed body.

"I fished my gun out from behind my back. You see, I was feeling funny again. Then I started to slide one foot over the edge of the bunk, always with my eyes on that shadow. Now I swear I didn't make the sound of a pin dropping, but I had no more than moved a muscle when that shadowed thing twisted itself around in a flash — and there on the floor before me was the profile of a man's head, upside down, listening — a man's head with a tail of hair."

McCord got up hastily and stepped over in front of the stateroom door, where he bent down and scratched a match.

"See," he said, holding the tiny flame above a

splintered scar on the boards. "You wouldn't think a man would be fool enough to shoot at a shadow?"

He came back and sat down.

"It seemed to me all hell had shaken loose. You've no idea, Ridgeway, the rumpus a gun raises in a box like this. I found out afterward the slug ricochetted into the galley, bringing down a couple of pans — and that helped. Oh, yes, I got out of here quick enough. I stood there, half out of the companion, with my hands on the hatch and the gun between them, and my shadow running off across the top of the house shivering before my eyes like a dry leaf. There wasn't a whisper of sound in the world — just the pale water floating past and the sails towering up like a pair of twittering ghosts. And everything that crazy colour —

"Well, in a minute I saw it, just abreast of the mainmast, crouched down in the shadow of the weather rail, sneaking off forward very slowly. This time I took a good long sight before I let go. Did you ever happen to see black-powder smoke in the moonlight? It puffed out perfectly round, like a big, pale balloon, this did, and for a second something was bounding through it — without a sound, you understand — something a shade solider than the smoke and big as a cow, it looked to me. It passed from the weather side to the lee and ducked behind the sweep of the mainsail like *that* — " McCord snapped his thumb and forefinger under the light.

"Go on," I said. "What did you do then?"

McCord regarded me for an instant from beneath his lids, uncertain. His fist hung above the table. "You're — " He hesitated, his lips working vacantly. A forefinger came out of the fist and gesticulated before my face. "If you're laughing, why, damn me, I'll — "

"Go on," I repeated. "What did you do then?"

"I followed the thing." He was still watching me sullenly. "I got up and went forward along the roof of the house, so as to have an eye on either rail. You understand, this business had to be done with. I kept straight along. Every shadow I wasn't absolutely sure of I *made* sure of — point-blank. And I rounded the thing up at the very stern — sitting on the butt of the bowsprit, Ridgeway, washing her yellow face under the moon. I didn't make any bones about it this time. I put the bad end of that gun against the scar on her head and squeezed the trigger. It snicked on an empty shell. I tell you a fact; I was almost deafened by the report that didn't come.

"She followed me aft. I couldn't get away from her. I went and sat on the wheel-box and she came and sat on the edge of the house, facing me. And there we stayed for upward of an hour, without moving. Finally she went over and stuck her paw in the water-pan I'd set out for her; then she raised her head and looked at me and yawled. At sundown there'd been two quarts of water in that pan. You wouldn't think a cat could get away with two quarts of water in — "

He broke off again and considered me with a sort of weary defiance.

"What's the use?" He spread out his hands in a gesture of hopelessness. "I knew you wouldn't believe it when I started. You *couldn't*. It would be a kind of blasphemy against the sacred institution of pavements. You're too damn smug, Ridgeway. I can't shake you. You haven't sat two days and two nights, keeping your eyes open by sheer teeth-gritting, until they got used to it and wouldn't shut any more. When

I tell you I found that yellow thing snooping around the davits, and three bights off the boat-fall loosened out, plain on deck — you grin behind your collar. When I tell you she padded off forward and evaporated — flickered back to hell and hasn't been seen since, then — why, you explain to yourself that I'm drunk. I tell you — " He jerked his head back abruptly and turned to face the companionway, his lips still apart. He listened so for a moment, then he shook himself out of it and went on:

"I tell you, Ridgeway, I've been over this hulk with a foot-rule. There's not a cubic inch I haven't accounted for, not a plank I — "

This time he got up and moved a step toward the companion, where he stood with his head bent forward and slightly to the side. After what might have been twenty seconds of this he whispered, "Do you hear?"

Far and far away down the reach a ferry-boat lifted its infinitesimal wail, and then the silence of the night river came down once more, profound and inscrutable. A corner of the wick above my head sputtered a little — that was all.

"Hear what?" I whispered back. He lifted a cautious finger toward the opening.

"Somebody. Listen."

The man's faculties must have been keyed up to the pitch of his nerves, for to me the night remained as voiceless as a subterranean cavern. I became intensely irritated with him; within my mind I cried out against this infatuated pantomime of his. And then, of a sudden, there was a sound — the dying rumour of a ripple, somewhere in the outside darkness, as though an object had been let into the water with extreme care.

"You heard?"

I nodded. The ticking of the watch in my vest pocket came to my ears, shucking off the leisurely seconds, while McCord's finger-nails gnawed at the palms of his hands. The man was really sick. He wheeled on me and cried out, "My God! Ridgeway — why don't we go out?"

I, for one, refused to be a fool. I passed him and climbed out of the opening; he followed far enough to lean his elbows on the hatch, his feet and legs still within the secure glow of the cabin.

"You see, there's nothing." My wave of assurance was possibly a little overdone.

"Over there," he muttered, jerking his head toward the shore lights. "Something swimming."

I moved to the corner of the house and listened.

"River thieves," I argued. "The place is full of — "

"*Ridgeway. Look behind you!*"

Perhaps it is the pavements — but no matter; I am not ordinarily a jumping sort. And yet there was something in the quality of that voice beyond my shoulder that brought the sweat stinging through the pores of my scalp even while I was in the act of turning.

A cat sat there on the hatch, expressionless and immobile in the gloom.

I did not say anything. I turned and went below. McCord was there already, standing on the farther side of the table. After a moment or so the cat followed and sat on her haunches at the foot of the ladder and stared at us without winking.

"I think she wants something to eat," I said to McCord.

He lit a lantern and went out into the galley. Returning with a chunk of salt beef, he threw it into the farther corner. The cat went over and began to tear at it, her muscles playing with convulsive shadow-lines under the sagging yellow hide.

And now it was she who listened, to something beyond the reach of even McCord's faculties, her neck stiff and her ears flattened. I looked at McCord and found him brooding at the animal with a sort of listless malevolence. "*Quick!* She has kittens somewhere about." I shook his elbow sharply. "When she starts, now — "

"You don't seem to understand," he mumbled. "It wouldn't be any use."

She had turned now and was making for the ladder with the soundless agility of her race. I grasped McCord's wrist and dragged him after me, the lantern banging against his knees. When we came up the cat was already amidships, a scarcely discernible shadow at the margin of our lantern's ring. She stopped and looked back at us with her luminous eyes, appeared to hesitate, uneasy at our pursuit of her, shifted here and there with quick, soft bounds, and stopped to fawn with her back arched at the foot of the mast. Then she was off with an amazing suddenness into the shadows forward.

'Lively now!" I yelled at McCord. He came pounding along behind me, still protesting that it was of no use. Abreast of the foremast I took the lantern from him to hold above my head.

"You see," he complained, peering here and there over the illuminated deck. "I tell you, Ridgeway, this thing — " But my eyes were in another quarter, and I slapped him on the shoulder.

"An engineer — an engineer to the core," I cried at him. "Look aloft, man."

Our quarry was almost to the cross-trees, clambering up the shrouds with a smartness no sailor has ever come to, her yellow body, cut by the moving shadows of the ratlines, a queer sight against the mat of the night. McCord closed his mouth and opened it again for two words: "By gracious!" The following instant he had the lantern and was after her. I watched him go up above my head — a ponderous, swaying climber into the sky — come to the cross-trees, and squat there with his knees clamped around the mast. The clear star of the lantern shot this way and that for a moment, then it disappeared, and in its place there sprang out a bag of yellow light, like a fire-balloon at anchor in the heavens. I could see the shadows of his head and hands moving monstrously over the inner surface of the sail, and muffled exclamations without meaning came down to me. After a moment he drew out his head and called: "All right — they're here. Heads! there below!"

I ducked at his warning, and something spanked on the planking a yard from my feet. I stepped over to the vague blur on the deck and picked up a slipper — a slipper covered with some woven straw stuff and soled with a matted felt, perhaps a half-inch thick. Another struck somewhere abaft the mast, and then McCord reappeared above and began to stagger down the shrouds. Under his left arm he hugged a curious assortment of litter, a sheaf of papers, a brace of revolvers, a gray kimono, and a soiled apron.

"Well," he said when he had come to deck, "I feel like a man who has gone to hell and come back again. You know I'd come to the place where I really believed that about the cat. When you think of it — By gracious! we haven't come so far from the jungle, after all."

We went aft and below and sat down at the table as we had been. McCord broke a prolonged silence.

"I'm sort of glad he got away — poor cuss! He's probably climbing up a wharf this minute, shivering and scared to death. Over toward the gas-tanks, by the way he was swimming. By gracious! now that the world's turned over straight again, I feel I could sleep a solid week. Poor cuss! can you imagine him, Ridgeway — "

"Yes," I broke in. "I think I can. He must have lost his nerve when he made out your smoke and shinnied up there to stow away, taking the ship's papers with him. He would have attached some profound importance to them — remember, the 'barbarian,' eight thousand miles from home. Probably couldn't read a word. I suppose the cat followed him — the traditional source of food. He must have wanted water badly."

"I should say! He wouldn't have taken the chances he did."

"Well," I announced, "at any rate, I can say it now — there's another 'mystery of the sea' gone to pot."

McCord lifted his heavy lids.

"No," he mumbled. "The mystery is that a man

who has been to sea all his life could sail around for three days with a man bundled up in his top and not know it. When I think of him peeking down at me — and playing off that damn cat — probably without realizing it — scared to death — by gracious! Ridgeway, there was a pair of funks aboard this craft, eh? Wow — yow — I could sleep — "

"I should think you could."

McCord did not answer.

"By the way," I speculated. "I guess you were right about Björnsen, McCord — that is, his fooling with the foretop. He must have been caught all of a bunch, eh?"

Again McCord failed to answer. I looked up mildly surprised, and found his head hanging back over his chair and his mouth opened wide. He was asleep.

IX. Letter to Sura — Pliny, the Younger

Our leisure furnishes me with the opportunity of learning from you, and you with that of instructing me. Accordingly, I particularly wish to know whether you think there exist such things as phantoms, possessing an appearance peculiar to themselves, and a certain supernatural power, or that mere empty delusions receive a shape from our fears. For my part, I am led to believe in their existence, especially by what I hear happened to Curtius Rufus. While still in humble circumstances and obscure, he was a hanger-on in the suit of the Governor of Africa. While pacing the colonnade one afternoon, there appeared to him a female form of superhuman size and beauty. She informed the terrified man that she was "Africa," and had come to foretell future events; for that he would go to Rome, would fill offices of state there, and would even return to that same province with the highest powers, and die in it. All which things were fulfilled. Moreover, as he touched at Carthage, and was disembarking from his ship, the same form is said to have presented itself to him on the shore. It is certain that, being seized with illness, and auguring the future from the past and misfortune from his previous prosperity, he himself abandoned all hope of life, though none of those about him despaired.

Is not the following story again still more appalling and not less marvellous? I will relate it as it was received by me:

There was at Athens a mansion, spacious and commodious, but of evil repute and dangerous to health. In the dead of night there was a noise as of iron, and, if you listened more closely, a clanking of chains was heard, first of all from a distance, and afterward hard by. Presently a spectre used to appear, an ancient man sinking with emaciation and squalor, with a long beard and bristly hair, wearing shackles on his legs and fetters on his hands, and shaking them. Hence the inmates, by reason of their fears, passed miserable and horrible nights in sleeplessness. This want of sleep was followed by disease, and, their terrors increasing, by death. For in the daytime as well, though the apparition had departed, yet a reminiscence of it flitted before their eyes, and their dread outlived its cause. The mansion was accordingly deserted, and condemned to solitude, was entirely abandoned to the dreadful ghost. However, it was advertised, on the chance of someone, ignorant of the fearful curse attached to it, being willing to buy or to rent it. Athenodorus, the philosopher, came to Athens and read the advertisement. When he had been informed of the terms, which were so low as to appear suspicious, he made inquiries, and learned the whole of the particulars. Yet none the less on that account, nay, all the more readily, did he rent the house. As evening began to draw on, he ordered a sofa to be set for himself in the front part of the house, and called for his notebooks, writing implements, and a light. The whole of his servants he dismissed to the interior apartments, and for himself applied his soul, eyes, and hand to composition, that his mind might not, from want of occupation, picture to itself the phantoms of which he had heard, or any empty terrors. At the commencement there was the universal silence of night. Soon the shaking of irons and the clanking of chains was heard, yet he never raised his eyes nor slackened his pen, but hardened his soul and deadened his ears by its help. The noise grew and approached: now it seemed to be heard at the door, and next inside the door. He looked round, beheld and recognized the figure he had been told of. It was standing and signalling to him with its finger, as though inviting him. He, in reply, made a sign with his hand that it should wait a moment, and applied himself afresh to his tablets and pen. Upon this the figure kept rattling its chains over his head as he wrote. On looking round again, he saw it making the same signal as before, and without delay took up a light and followed it. It moved with a slow step, as though oppressed by its chains, and, after turning into the courtyard of the house, vanished suddenly and left his company. On being thus left to himself, he marked the spot with some grass and leaves which he plucked. Next day he applied to the magistrates, and urged them to have the spot in question dug up. There were found there some bones attached to and intermingled with fetters; the body to which they had belonged, rotted away by time and the soil, had abandoned them thus naked and corroded to the chains. They were collected and interred at the public expense, and the house was ever afterward free from the spirit, which had obtained due sepulture.

The above story I believe on the strength of those who affirm it. What follows I am myself in a position to affirm to others. I have a freedman, who is not without some knowledge of letters. A younger brother of his was sleeping with him in the same bed. The latter dreamed he saw someone sitting on the couch, who approached a pair of scissors to his head, and even cut the hair from the crown of it. When day dawned he was found to be cropped round the crown, and his locks were discovered lying about. A very short time afterward a fresh occurrence of the same kind confirmed the truth of the former one. A lad of mine was sleeping, in company with several others, in the pages' apartment. There came through the windows (so he tells the story) two figures in white tunics, who cut his hair as he lay, and departed the way they came. In his case, too, daylight exhibited him shorn, and his locks scattered around. Nothing remarkable followed, except, perhaps, this, that I was not brought under accusation, as I should have been, if Domitian (in whose reign these events happened) had lived longer. For in his desk was found an information against me which had been presented by Carus; from which circumstance may be conjectured — inasmuch as it is the custom of accused persons to let their hair grow — that the cutting off of my slaves' hair was a sign of the danger which threatened me being averted.

I beg, then, that you will apply your great learning to this subject. The matter is one which deserves long and deep consideration on your part; nor am I, for my part, undeserving of having the fruits of your wisdom imparted to me. You may even argue on both sides (as your way is), provided you argue more forcibly on one side than the other, so as not to dismiss me in suspense and anxiety, when the very cause of my consulting you has been to have my doubts put an end to.

*****

THE END